Music Box Lady

Sep⁺ 11/95

To Bob,

Everyone enjoys a
little romance.
Hope you do too!

Jerry

Music Box Lady

Terrill A. Bodner

Northwest Publishing, Inc.
Salt Lake City, Utah

Music Box Lady

For information address: Northwest Publishing, Inc.
6906 South 300 West, Salt Lake City, Utah 84047
JC 10 06 94
Edited by S.J. Davis

PRINTING HISTORY
First Printing 1995

ISBN: 1-56901-716-6

NPI books are published by Northwest Publishing, Incorporated,
6906 South 300 West, Salt Lake City, Utah 84047.
The name "NPI" and the "NPI" logo are trademarks belonging to
Northwest Publishing, Incorporated.

PRINTED IN THE UNITED STATES OF AMERICA.
10 9 8 7 6 5 4 3 2 1

One

"Good morning, ladies and gentlemen. I'm Michael Ryan, the man you've all been waiting for."

Vanessa Lawrence straightened her shoulders, giving them a soft shrug as she settled in the front row seat she had chosen. Sensing she was being watched, Vanessa looked up to the raised platform as the buzz in the eighty-seat conference room dwindled to silence. The tall, well-dressed speaker in the navy suit flashed her a smile that stabbed at her heart, making her head swim and her blood race. For one piercing second she felt the resurgence of sexuality that she had thought was gone forever. As their eyes locked for an instant, she knew this handsome stranger before her was experiencing similar sensations.

Michael Ryan knew that just to get through the next two hours was going to be tough, realizing his concentration had already been broken by the intriguing young woman in front of him. He straightened his notes, giving the papers a sudden tap on the wooden podium. Michael forced himself to get back to his presentation, but not until he used the brief settling down period to focus on the tall, willowy blonde seated in front of him. He liked what he saw. She was certainly attractive in her business-like attire and neatly braided hair. His approving glance slid down the length of her shapely legs as he watched her tug at her short, black skirt. When she settled against the chair, he noticed in her left hand she held a gold pen, obviously poised to take notes. To his pleasure, he noted her well-manicured hand was devoid of any rings.

As he caught her gaze, he felt the sudden jolt of sexual desire rip through his body. The words "alone in a crowded room" took on new meaning as he fought the startling sensation that she felt the same thing he did. Somehow he knew she was going to be his, but for the moment he had a job to do, and he quickly focused his attention to the paperwork in front of him.

Vanessa fumbled to open the floral-covered notebook she held in her lap. She squirmed again to pull her neat black skirt closer to the top of her knees. The air-conditioning of the room made her shiver involuntarily in the thin cream silk blouse that she wore, or perhaps it was the sudden attack on her inner core that made her feel every nerve ending in her entire body awaken.

She should have taken a seat further back, she scolded herself, feeling that her normal business-like outfit was a little too revealing in the drafty atmosphere. She never enjoyed being on display, and the close scrutiny by the man who was to occupy the next two hours of her life made her very much aware of how she had avoided getting into many situations such as this over the past four years.

During the lecture she caught herself studying him standing before her, feeling a flush rise in her cheeks whenever he caught her eye as he spoke to the group. She was not one to eye a man's physique, but the overall appearance of the handsome man towering before her was having an effect on her that she had not felt in years.

His tanned hands adroitly poured a glass of water from the table beside the podium. Vanessa's eyes met his again, as if she had no control, like a gawking teenager staring at a movie star idol. She watched, mesmerized, as he moved the glass to his lips, swallowed his drink, the smooth motion of his throat as he consumed the water entrancing her.

She straightened, unconsciously licking her lips from the dryness she felt in her own mouth. The steely air of authority surrounded him as she listened to him continue with his presentation. He was well-spoken and very knowledgeable in business management.

His eyes were a cool steel gray, not a usual colour for someone with such fine features. His warm brown hair was streaked with lighter highlights, possibly gray. Vanessa touched her own lips with the back of her hand, wondering how the sensation of his mustache rubbing against her smooth upper lip would feel. Remembering her reason for attending the seminar, Vanessa took her eyes off him reluctantly for a moment, and jotted down a few points she wanted to look into further.

After presenting all his points on how to successfully manage a small business, Michael opened the floor for questions, taking up the last half-hour of the seminar.

"I'd be happy to answer any of your questions, if you'd like to see me individually. You've been very receptive and I thank you." Applause. The room cleared out quickly, with most of the participants heading for their normal Thursday morning activities, leaving Michael sorting his papers and stuffing them into his black leather briefcase. He glanced toward the floor, his heart pounding excitedly as he realized he did not have to chase after the blonde beauty who tantalized him. He tried to control the tingling sensation that rose up his spine as he waited for her to approach him.

Vanessa touched her perfectly braided blonde hair with a fleeting graze of her hand, and stepped with practiced ease toward him. Her pulse quickened as he greeted her from his position on the raised platform. He displayed a most charming smile, as Vanessa felt him watching her every move. She was terribly aware of the desire mounting inside her, and she fought to control the rising warmth that penetrated deep in her belly.

"Mr. Ryan, I…"

"Call me Michael," he said, stepping from behind the podium, still remaining on the elevated platform. He extended his big, tanned hand to greet her.

She accepted his outreached hand and took it in her smooth palm. His grip was strong, his hands rough. She was surprised at the roughness. Not the hands of an accountant, she thought, making her wonder what else he must do for a living.

"Michael." His name rolled off her tongue eloquently, making her expose the straight white teeth through parted lips. The thought of giving him her name escaped her as she hurried with her reason to approach him. "I have a question about the incentive program you outlined earlier."

"Shoot." He crouched down to face her, his leg muscles flexed tightly against the navy wool pant legs.

Vanessa swallowed, giving herself a moment to recapture the question she had wanted to ask before his sudden shift to meet her eye to eye brought the scent of his cologne wafting gently around her. "Is there any way to compensate an employee for loyalty, even if her store is not one of the profitable ones?"

"Yes, there are several incentive programs in existence. What is it that you do?"

"I own a small chain of music box stores. Perhaps you've heard of it. The Ballerina Music Box Company." His eyes intrigued her. Never before had she seen anyone with such gray eyes, so clear and intense. Her eyes strayed, following his free hand that raised to smooth his short brown hair which showed the tell-tale signs of premature graying. She struggled to control her inner composure as she waited for him to answer.

"No, I've never heard of it, but that sounds like a good business for you. Music boxes are for pretty girls." He flashed her a brilliant, straight-toothed smile, making the corners of his eyes crinkle.

She blushed furiously, wishing she could control the rising heat within her. She never considered herself beautiful, but the sound of his words caressed her heart with their golden touch. She smiled serenely, biting her tongue at the same time. It had taken four years of struggling to learn the business the hard way, from the ground up, but she had succeeded in making it very profitable through long hours of study and practice to manage the chain of stores her husband had started when they were married. She had fought hard to erase the 'poor little rich girl' image that was cast upon her when she became the sole owner of the business. She now commanded the respect that being the owner of a successful enterprise dictated, and she enjoyed the feeling of power it brought to her life, but she wasn't about to defend her position to this stranger before her right now.

"Perhaps you could come by the store and you can see for yourself how the business is run?" What is it with this guy, she wondered, that had her nervously hoping he would take her up on her offer. The tingling sensation in her lower abdomen that he caused just by standing in front of her unnerved her. "Then we can discuss the program in detail if you like."

"Sounds great. I have to fly to Vancouver early tomorrow but I have the rest of the day free, and besides, I am always interested in new businesses," he said. Something told him this woman was more complex than he originally thought and he had an uncontrollable urge to find out more about her.

The buttons of his jacket opened as he straightened up, exposing a taut, white shirt underneath. The open jacket enabled him to jump down from the stage. His tall frame loomed over her as he slipped his right hand easily into the well-fitting trousers. Looking deeply into her emerald-green eyes, he flustered her with his direct and sensual gaze.

"Okay, why not? I'm Vanessa, by the way." She extended her slim hand while holding the notebook tightly against her small breasts with the other as her stomach flip-flopped inside. "I hope you don't mind walking. It's just a few blocks from here and I try to walk wherever I can." She smiled again, her green eyes twinkling in the semi-lit auditorium.

"I'd love to," he replied, gathering the last of the papers and briefcase as he stretched up to the podium. Vanessa held back the urge to touch his taut torso, with rippling muscles marking the smoothness of the fabric. He looked like the outdoors type, but one could never be sure, she thought, smiling to herself. She headed toward the exit. He was right behind her and it surprised her to feel the warmth of his touch gently caress her back as he briefly put his powerful hand against her before he reached out to hold the door open for her.

It was a moderately warm day for May. It hadn't rained for over two weeks, but the clouds overhead were starting to darken as Michael and Vanessa chatted amicably while they walked the few blocks to the store. Vanessa tried to keep a little distance between them as they headed down the dusty city street. Just a whiff of his cologne was tantalizing enough. She sensed more than knew that she would have to be on her guard with this man if she was going to keep it strictly business. Past experience had taught her what men thought about a woman who was single and well-off like herself, and his charming smile made her aware of a need she had long ago repressed.

From the corner of his eye, Michael saw it coming before it registered on his brain. His reactions were smooth and swift.

"Look out," Michael shouted, pulling Vanessa hard against his solid chest just in time to save her from a head-on crash with a wild-haired teenager on a fast-rolling skateboard. Michael's muscular arms crushed her against him and she could feel his breath, warm against the fluff of her bangs. His height seemed overwhelming to her even though he only had a six-inch advantage over her. His scent reached her intensi-fied senses as she blinked, surprised and shaken at the near accident, and the sudden thrust into his arms caused her to nearly swoon in his embrace. She wanted to ask him what he wore, but she didn't dare. Whatever it was it intoxicated her. Had she been out of touch with the other sex for that long, she wondered.

Michael released her almost as quickly as he pulled her to him. The thought of tasting her lips as she stared up into his face made his masculinity soar as if his emotions were in a rapid crossfire of dangerous proportions. Did he really want Vanessa to know his true feelings toward her, or should he conceal his mounting desire until he gained her total trust?

The careless teen, already halfway down the block, was barely visible to Vanessa as she jerked her head to see what had rattled past them. "Thanks," she whispered. "I didn't even hear him coming." She pictured the catastrophe that could have resulted had the three of them collided on the sidewalk. Where was her head, anyway, she wondered. Certainly not in the present. She straightened her skirt as she tried to regain her composure.

"He was pretty fast, that's for sure." Michael continued to walk beside her in quiet ease, his heroic deed barely fazing him. The soft scent of her perfume wafted upwards as they reached their destination.

This time it was Vanessa's turn to notice the commotion before they reached the store. Her heart lurched at the thoughts that raced through her mind. Police were everywhere, redi-recting traffic, taking statements from passers-by. It took a moment for it to register before the high-pitched shriek escaped her lips.

"Oh, my God," she whispered, one hand covering her mouth as the other clutched Michael's arm as she hurried them toward the broken storefront window.

"Sorry, no one is allowed in," the clean-shaven young officer said, raising his hand to stop her from entering the taped off area.

"I'm Vanessa Lawrence, the owner. What has happened here?" she demanded, peering into the once-tidy store, now covered in broken glass and ceramic pieces of precious music boxes. Vanessa bit back tears as she pushed her way into the entrance. Michael followed silently behind her.

She wasn't prepared for what she saw next. Hovering over a shaking form draped in a blanket was another policeman, obviously uncomfortable with consoling a weeping woman. Vanessa rushed over to them as quickly as she could pick her way through the broken glass that was strewn all over the floor. She nearly fainted as she caught sight of the blood-stained cloth that her assistant, Janice, held to her forehead.

"Oh, Vanessa, I'm so sorry. I…"

"Hush, now," Vanessa said, standing shakily as she reached out to touch her friend gingerly. The sight of blood was not one of her favorite things and she swayed slightly, overwrought with the thought that one of her employees could have suffered such injury. This district was getting too run-down for her, she thought, remembering the near-collision with the skateboarder only moments ago. Michael guided her to a nearby chair, and set her down gently in it before taking over the situation.

Michael turned to the young policeman. "I think you might want to hear this," Michael began. He described the teenager on the skateboard as he watched the relief flood the young officer's face. Having something to go on satisfied the young man as he quickly took notes, and then excused himself after glancing at Michael and the two women, obviously assuming that they were now in good hands.

"Let's take a look at that," Michael said, bending down to Janice's level. Vanessa watched, fascinated, as he administered to Janice's abrasion. "Nothing serious, just a small gash. We better get you to a doctor, though." He glanced at Vanessa, assuring himself that she was recovering from the shock as well before he helped Janice to her feet.

"I'm okay, really," the petite dark-haired woman whispered. "Vanessa, I never even saw it coming. I was straightening the shelves when I heard the shatter. I didn't see anything."

"That's okay. You relax. I'll drive you to the hospital," Vanessa said as she again rose shakily from her chair.

Michael gave her a sharp glance. "You'll do no such thing. I'll drive her there, then come back for you. The store is going to be closed for a while and there really isn't anything more you can do. Call your insurance agent, and get the window replaced while I take Janice to the hospital. I'll be back shortly."

"But you don't know…" Vanessa was overwhelmed by the disastrous surroundings, as she tried to pick up the broken pieces of a favorite ballerina.

"Janice can direct me. Now, where are your keys?" He held out a strong hand in a way that she could not refuse him. He was still a stranger, but Vanessa was trapped. She couldn't leave the store until some things were taken care of. She felt responsible for Janice although she could never have seen anything like this coming. It was sheer vandalism. Vanessa's green eyes, brimming with unshed tears, met his cool, steel gray ones. She hesitated a moment before handing over the keys with shaky hands.

"It's in the back. A red sports car. Janice knows which one." She sighed as she surveyed the damage. Luckily, Janice was not hurt badly. Shards of glass lay everywhere. Vanessa went to work as soon as everyone cleared out. She arranged for glass replacement and insurance claims before she called the cleaning service. The police had all they needed and advised her to stay alert. The area was not what it used to be. She nodded before locking the door behind them.

Michael returned more quickly than Vanessa expected. She jumped at the intrusion of the hard knock at her back door. She peered through the peephole, unaware she was holding her breath until she recognized Michael. Letting out a sigh, she quickly unbolted the door and allowed him in. After receiving a brief report on Janice's condition, Vanessa began to relax a bit, relief flooding her face.

Michael surveyed the surroundings as he stepped inside her store. The soft rose-coloured walls reflected the femininity of the customers who were the recipients of most of the objects that were for sale. Michael's eyes scanned the room, finding the surroundings pleasing, although somewhat too dainty for his taste.

Vanessa led him to the 'staff only' door a few feet away from Janice's neat desk. "Here we are," Vanessa said, touching him gently on his jacket sleeve. There was fire in her fingers, he felt, as he was jolted out of his thoughts.

He followed her through the long hallway, neatly decorated with pictures of ballerinas. Most of them were of beautiful little girls wearing pink or white tutus, their faces somber in the concentration of the pose. Looking closer, one could see that each one was standing on the lid of a delicately carved music box.

"Who decorated your hallway?" he asked, stopping in front of one of the prints to admire it. The frame was a gleaming brass, accented by the stark whiteness of the background of the photographs.

Vanessa stopped at her door. "Janice and I did."

"I like it. Are music boxes a favorite of yours? You must have a lot of them at home."

Vanessa looked at her hands as her stomach tightened. She had never asked Mark why he hadn't brought her any of the beautiful little boxes, although now she never considered buying the ones that were her particular favorites. It would not be the same as a gift. "No, I don't," she answered curtly as she pushed open the door to her office.

Noting the abruptness in her voice, Michael chose not to pursue the topic. She seemed to get her ire up very quickly, and he had no intention of ruining what might be a perfect liaison if he played his cards right.

The room was not what he expected after reading the gilded lettering that identified the president's office. His gray eyes softened as he stood in the middle of the large, tastefully decorated room. He scanned the walls, his eyes catching the sight of the side wall that was lined with a large bookshelf containing many of the latest hardcover bestsellers.

"Would you like to sit down?" Vanessa said, indicating his choice of a plush burgundy velvet or black leather love seat placed one on either side of her huge antique oak desk.

He accepted the leather one, his long muscular legs bending as he tugged at his pant legs. Placing his cupped hands between his knees, he leaned forward. She sat down in her chair, feeling slightly warm as she secretly admired his broad shoulders, lean build and tanned good looks.

"So this is the Ballerina Music Box Company. You must be very proud of your accomplishments. The decor, minus the mess out there, is extremely enticing to a female clientele."

"Thank you. Customer service is our main function. When we give that, the selling part comes naturally. But the majority of our clients are men, looking for something for a woman. The decor tells them that this is what she would like." She picked up the pencil that was left on top of the daily sales ledger.

"Yes, I agree." His eyes followed her every move behind the big desk. And there was more that came naturally, if you let it, he mused, keeping his smoldering look barely hidden from her.

Vanessa tried to control the thoughts that raced through her mind. The two of them were alone in the room, and his presence was becoming overpowering. Afraid of what could happen behind closed doors, she tried to get back on track with the meeting.

"You can see why I want to start an incentive program. The staff are so good, and it's because of them that we have made a turn-around in the last year. I feel the future of this company is in the hands of the employees." Her love for her staff and the interest she held in her company clearly showed in her voice.

"You're right in wanting to reward your staff for their efforts. Many companies are just starting to set up incentive programs for their employees." He watched her lean back in her chair, twirling the pencil in her one hand.

"Incentives used to be just for upper management, and some companies filtered it down to middle management," he continued, holding her interest. "When the recession hit in 1981 that was when all these types of plans were stopped by most retailers. You're smart to start thinking about this now. It's the way of the nineties if your company really wants to succeed." He stretched his long arms across the back of the smooth leather couch.

Vanessa shifted in her seat, growing uncomfortably aware of the stirring inside her as she fought the desire to settle on the love seat beside him.

"I've read a few articles on it lately." She opened her bottom drawer, pulled a file, and placed it on her desk. She gestured for him to look at it.

He rose quickly, crossing the short distance that separated him from the tantalizing woman in front of him. He was certainly impressed with her business knowledge and keen market sense.

She studied the strong, tanned hands as he picked up the top article and leafed through it. Her pulse quickened as she imagined those very hands touching her in the most intimate places.

"Is this where you got your ideas?"

"Yes, and I've been considering them just this last year. We are finally showing a profit. It's been a struggle the three years before this one. But the staff has been so good," she said hesitating.

"And you feel you want to reward the loyal ones."

"Yes. Can you help?" she asked, point-blank.

Taking in the intense seriousness in her eyes, the round fullness of her tightly pursed lips, he nodded. He smiled down at her, seeing her face warm to his positive answer.

"If you'd like, I could help you set it up. From what you've told me of your company, it wouldn't take long to design the program." He was already forming the plan in his mind when she nodded in agreement.

She smiled, straight teeth glistening in the late afternoon light that filtered through the lacy curtains. "Keep your receipts to give to Janice when you are through," she started before he interrupted.

"I'll help. You don't have to pay my way," he added, sounding offended. His defensive position highlighted the strength in his jaw as he raised his chin slightly in a look of defiance.

"I am quite capable of hiring you for your services," she said, before turning a bright shade of pink as she realized too late the double entendre.

He leaned forward, staring intently into her eyes. A quirky smile played at his lips. "I'm sure you are, Vanessa," he said in a husky voice, "but I insist. I really would like to learn more about a company like yours. It could prove beneficial to my business as well. Let's just consider it research on my part, okay?"

"Oh, all right, for research." Vanessa wondered whether she might feel she owed him a favor in return, but since he seemed to be genuinely interested in the business, she cast the hint of indebtedness aside for the moment.

It was well into the afternoon, and the sound of her stomach rumbling made her wrap her arms across her stomach to quell the noise.

"It sounds like you are as hungry as I am. How about getting something to eat? There's not much left to show me of the business. I think you've given me all I'll need," Michael said, indicating the pile of papers Vanessa had copied for him while he tended to Janice at the hospital. He was amazed she could carry on after the shock of earlier this morning, and a growing respect for his blonde fixation became more apparent as he watched her.

Acutely embarrassed to have him hear the rumblings, Vanessa nodded, taking a few paces to step in front of him, leading the way to the exit.

"I know a nice spot," she said, stopping to lock the back door before heading to her little sports car. Michael opened the car door with the keys he neglected to return to her earlier.

"I'll drive," he said, ushering her around to the passenger side before she could protest. The touch of his fingers on her arm sparked a rush of heat that created a tingle all the way up her arm. Vanessa blushed at her reaction, ducking her head quickly to avoid him noticing her suddenly flushed face.

Upon reaching the restaurant, Michael opened the door for her, gesturing that she should enter first. The succulent aroma of herbs and garlic filled the crowded room. Waiting to be seated, Vanessa stole a glimpse of his handsome face as he surveyed the tiny dining room. Cozy tables for two were neatly tucked into the corners of the room, and lining the wall against the windows. The blue-checkered tablecloths finished off the interior, matching the white trim and blue painted walls.

"You haven't given me your life story yet, you know," he said after the pretty young waitress seated them in a secluded corner.

"What do you want to know?" she asked. "I already told you I'm a widow, now running my husband's business. There's not much more to me than that," she stated flatly, in the matter-of-fact manner she had developed over the last four years of business dealings she had found herself thrown into.

"What about your hopes, your dreams? Is this all you want out of life, to work?" His eyes followed the contours of her face, and he had to curb the urge to stroke the smooth skin.

She settled into her chair before answering, giving herself a few seconds to arrange her purse and notebook under her chair. His unsettling gray eyes held hers. She knew it wasn't just his eyes that intrigued her. His long, muscular legs contributed to his six-foot-two build nicely. And his broad shoulders. She forced herself to get her mind back to his question.

"I never really thought about it. When I was a little girl, I always wanted to raise horses, but...things changed. I moved west. I met Mark."

"Who's Mark?" he asked, as his eyes met Vanessa's with

such openness that she had to shift her gaze from his. She glanced down at the table again, suddenly unnerved by such a personal question. The flash of guilt she experienced whenever she realized she was enjoying herself appeared once more. She hadn't felt the guilt for being the survivor of the accident much over the past year, but it had taken almost three grueling years of hard work and determination to put her life back together again.

Michael leaned forward to hear her barely audible whisper. "He was my husband. He died in a car accident."

"I'm sorry. That must have been awful for you." He leaned back in his chair. The pain that he had caused to be resurfaced in such a vulnerable yet beautiful woman showed in her face.

"That was four years ago, but I'm okay now." She smiled slightly, her lips pressed tightly together as she maintained her control. It was easier to talk about the accident to a total stranger now, but Vanessa recalled the struggle she had endured to get her life back together after Mark died. The look in her eyes reflected a haunting that was still apparent to anyone keen enough to notice.

Michael waited, as if unsure of what to say.

Aware of his discomfort, Vanessa continued. "It was Mark who started The Ballerina Music Box Company, and he struggled with it for six years before he died. It has only been the last four years that I became involved in it. I guess you could say I was thrown into the business." She gave a light laugh, smiling at him as the waitress approached, breaking the solemnity of the moment.

The pretty, dark-haired waitress offered to take their drink orders, paying particular attention to Michael while placing the menus in front of them. Vanessa felt a sudden pang of jealousy when he flirted back with the young woman. Trying to hide her irrational reaction, Vanessa settled for a glass of the white house wine. Michael ordered the same. After all, she had planned on buying him dinner in payment for all his help earlier, and she had to admit to herself she intended to find out everything she could from this handsome, virile man.

Michael's eyes explored the oval contour of her face; she had smooth cheekbones, highlighted through the adept use of makeup. He noticed the bright gold speckles in her glowing green eyes. The silky blonde hair that had been viciously tied back in a sleek braid now had soft wisps curling around the forehead covered with perky bangs.

"It's a nice place here," Michael said, trying to break the silence that crept between them.

"Yes, it is…" her voice trailed off, as she glanced down at the lace centerpiece, gently fingering the softly edged fabric. "I used to come here more often, but since Mark died…" she said, quietly, suddenly realizing it had been over four years since she had set foot in the little restaurant.

Michael reached across the table to touch her hand. She pulled it back instinctively but not before she could escape the heat that zapped through her fingers and up her arm. If just a touch from him could do this to her, what was in store for her if she were to let him pursue his obvious desire to have her as his own?

"Do I make you nervous?" he inquired, watching her blush as she tried to escape the piercing dark eyes.

"N-no, I…I've been having a little trouble falling asleep lately. That's usually what happens when I stay up late working on something." She moved the hand he had touched to the nape of her neck, trying to gently rub out the tension that was building inside her.

"What were you working on?"

"This incentive program. I really want it to be a success." She needed his help, but didn't want to be indebted to him for more than she already was. And she didn't know how tight a schedule he had. She was unsure if it was a smart idea to continue the pretense of having him help her with her work. After all, she knew she wanted him passionately, and the inner turmoil inside her gnawed at her gut. He was not from around here, and she knew it would only be an affair of the heart if she would let it. The fear she felt as she admitted she wanted him made her quake inside.

Michael had only the rest of the day left before he had to fly to Vancouver in the morning for his next seminar, and he intended to spend more than the day with this tall, sensuous blonde. He glanced at her hands, soft and smooth, as she raised the wine glass to her delicate, pouty lips. Just the thought of her touching him in all the right places made him shift uncomfortably in his seat.

Dinner arrived, but curiously, she found she was not hungry. As she watched him dig into his meal, she thought he did not suit the image of self-made businessman he seemed to be trying to project. Glancing at the strong hands breaking a piece of pita bread, she again noticed the hands of a working man. They were not the clean, manicured hands of an accountant-type with the rough callused palms lined with dirt that could never come out no matter how much one scrubbed. These were definitely working hands, like the hands of her father who spent his entire life farming on the east coast.

Michael looked up from his meal, noticing she was not eating. "I thought you were starving," he said between swallows. His strong hand gestured toward her plate, still grasping his empty fork.

His gray eyes met hers, and she coloured slightly. She glanced down at her plate, wondering why he had this effect on her. Nothing had been touched, as he had so keenly observed.

"I...I was wondering what you actually do for a living," she asked brazenly.

He looked at her, a puzzled expression on his tanned face.

"Your hands," she said, pointing, "they're not businessman's hands." She peered into the entrancing depths of his gray eyes.

Michael flashed a toothy grin under his mustache, his lips curling up into a crooked smile, making the deep, vertical lines in his cheeks appear deeper. He had sex appeal, all right. Vanessa studied his handsome face as he explained.

"Right you are, Vanessa. Most of my time is spent in Blue River, running a small ranch." He leaned back in the wooden chair. Vanessa's eyes strayed from his face, following the expanse of chest that stretched between his massive shoulders. Her heart pounded faster, making it almost impossible for her to focus back to the subject. "I grew up with my grandparents from the age of twelve. Gram was the only one who understood me, and I was lucky to have her. Gramps taught me the ways of the land."

Vanessa straightened in her chair. "How did you get your business background then?" A cowboy management consultant, she thought. What a combination.

"Gram didn't want me to waste my life on the ranch so she socked away every cent she had so I could go to a university. I earned my degree in business administration, but when Gramps died, I returned to the ranch. I missed it when I was away, and Gram needed me."

She watched his expression soften as he talked about his grandparents. She thought how hard it must have been to be orphaned at the age of twelve. Her parents were still alive, living on a farm in Guysborough, Nova Scotia. A pang of longing coursed through her, remembering the better days of sunny summers spent in carefree childhood bliss. She made a mental note to call them soon.

"How are you and your grandmother doing now?" she asked.

"Gram died six months after Gramps…"

Vanessa found herself wanting to console him, reaching out across the table to touch his arm, the heat of contact flashing through her fingers.

"I'm sorry," she said. The sadness in her green eyes reflected the pain she herself endured in her own loss.

"Thanks." He was silent for a moment, as he looked down at his almost empty plate. He raised his head, the soft brown forelock framing his smoky eyes. Her eyes met his for a long moment. Her heart picked up its steady pace, sending a warm rush through her, filling her mind with images of the two of them alone together.

She was not aware she was holding her breath until she

broke the tension-filled silence that grew between them as they watched each other. "I should be getting home soon," she said hastily. He was getting under her skin, and she wasn't sure she was ready for what she suspected he wanted, or what she herself desired.

The waitress presented the bill to Michael as Vanessa protested. The pretty young woman ignored her complaint, smiling and chatting to him as if Vanessa did not exist. Vanessa stood back, allowing Michael to charm the waitress a moment before he directed his attention back to her. Was it just his appearance that attracted her as it seemed to attract other women around her, or was there something deeper in this handsome stranger who had just waltzed into her life? Vanessa mused over the thought while Michael helped her with her coat.

Michael held the door for her again, admiring her every move. She was definitely a lady. The way she held her head high gave her the appearance of a true business woman. Her business sense was uncanny considering she had only spent the last four years in it. A slow respect grew inside him for the sensuous creature he fantasized about during his lecture.

"Well, I guess I should be going," she said, not knowing what else to say. It had been a pleasant dinner, but if she did not end their evening on a business note, she knew she would have trouble saying no if he asked her to join him for a nightcap. Or do men still do that, she wondered, feeling the years of empty nights and lack of social contact creep up on her. It was not that she did not go out with men. Just not with any that interested her the way he did.

"Would you care to go for a drink, before you head home? It's going to be a long night for me," he said, exaggerating a sad expression.

She could not help but laugh at his lost puppy face. "Trying to make me feel guilty for something you volunteered to do, are you?" she asked, flirtatiously, her heart soaring unexpectedly.

"Is it working?" His gray eyes stunned her with their cool depth as they gazed into hers.

She tried to decline his offer, but the firm rejection that formed in her head refused to be spoken by the softly-rounded lips that gave her response. "Yes, I guess so. There's a quiet dance lounge just off the lobby, I think. Why not stop there?"

"Sounds good," he said, leaning against the counter, as he finished signing the bill.

She walked beside him, feeling the warmth of his body against her, relishing the feelings that laid so dormant in her for so long. He was having quite a nice effect on her, she knew, but wouldn't admit to him. Their afternoon spent in the close quarters of her office going over her books brought a familiarity between them that made her ache for companionship on a much longer term.

Michael led her to a quiet corner. The band was playing easy-listening tunes from the seventies and eighties. Vanessa settled into the plush velvet chair, relaxing to the gentle flow of music. It had been too long since she enjoyed herself as much. The gentle touch on her hand made her jump.

"Thanks for asking me to dinner," he said. "I really enjoy your company, you know." His voice softly caressed her with his gentle words.

Vanessa felt the warmth creep up her slender neck, thankful the room was dark. She had been warm all evening, even though the ceiling fan spun overhead in the restaurant, making a cool breeze blow the tropical leaves above their table.

"It was nice to go out. I haven't done it for so long."

"Then you're not seeing anyone at the moment?" he asked. His gray eyes focused intently on her, making her feel very much aware how long it had been since she was out alone with a man. The dinner get-togethers with her sister always contained an evening of entertaining some eligible male friend of the family, but no one Vanessa was ever interested in.

"No one, really. I keep very busy with my work."

Michael listened to her, leaning forward to hear her over the relaxing hum of the music.

"How about you?" she heard herself asking.

"No one at the moment. But things could change," he said, smiling, his teeth flashing in the dimness. "Would you care to dance?" he asked, pulling her to her feet as the band started a slow waltz.

Vanessa started to protest, but the sensation that coursed through her body, upon the impact of his torso on hers made her melt. The scent of his cologne mixed with his own personal male smell was intoxicating.

He held her firmly, looking down upon her from his vantage point of a few inches since she was wearing the high heels she had switched to at the office. Gently he moved his hand back and forth across her shoulders and back. Her mind was confused, but her body knew exactly what was happening. It had been too long since anyone had touched her as he did. As the music ended, he reached out and smoothed her cheek with a slow stroking of his strong hand. She raised her own hand to cover his. Their eyes met and held for a long moment. He brushed her mouth with his lips and she could feel excitement and panic rising up together, each emotion fighting to surface first.

He was making her breathless with his gentle caresses, and she had to fight her rising feelings to keep in control. How could she possibly feel those things for a man she had known for less than a day, she wondered.

Michael felt the tension in her suddenly stiff body. The next song started almost immediately as he walked her to their table. He had wanted to ask her to dance with him again, to move to the sexy rhythm until she regained her fluidity, but he suspected that he was going to have to take it slow with this music box lady if he wanted a chance to make her his.

She tried to regain some composure, straightening her skirt as she sat down. He was having such an heady effect on her, she was beginning to think it was the wine. She tried to remember how many glasses she had, but she had lost track by the time dessert arrived. If she was going to handle his overtures she had better behave herself, she decided resolutely. She had noticed his firm maleness pressed against her as they danced. She didn't think she could have that effect on a man, especially one that she didn't know well.

"How about going for a walk?" Michael suggested. "It's getting warm in here, and I think the fresh air would do us some good." He brushed the side of his head with an open palm, straightening the gray-streaked hair that he seemed to know was out of place.

"I think you're right," she said, thankful for an excuse to escape the overpowering hold he was beginning to have on her. She reached for her purse and notebook under her chair. Noticing his left foot tapping nervously against the table leg, she felt a little better. He may not be as calm and collected as he appeared on the outside. Goodness knows she wasn't. She accepted his offer of a walk to take a little time to clear her head of the effects of the wine.

The darkness of the May evening had been cooled by the sudden shower that had fallen while they were dancing. The air was moist, refreshing, something Vanessa needed desperately.

They strolled together silently for three blocks, hips rubbing with every stride after Vanessa allowed him to link his arm protectively behind her back as she slipped hers through his. She could feel his warmth emanating through his suit jacket.

"Vanessa," he started, "I don't know what it is about you, but you have had quite an effect on me since I first saw you this morning." Vanessa was silent, listening. "I...I don't know how to handle it, I mean, what's going on here? I'm not the type to want a woman as badly as I want you right now." He stopped abruptly, swiveling her to face him.

Vanessa sucked in her breath audibly, her body tensing. The rain pattered down, softly dampening the fine planes of his face. The lamplight overhead cast a warm glow which reflected in his eyes.

"I…I'm having a little trouble handling it, too. It's not like me…I—" She was surprised by his sudden advance, pulling her close to him as they stood under the eaves of the art shop. He pressed his lips against hers, the moist heat of his mouth on hers feeling strange, tingly. Sparks zapped throughout her body, making her almost faint at the sudden impact he had on her. She hadn't been kissed like this ever, she realized, dazed by his impulsive move toward her as his hands gently pressed against her upper arms. He loosened his grip, allowing her arms to explore the broadness of his back as she returned his caress with more pent-up passion than she could control. The heat of his body crushing against hers made her own temperature rise considerably. He kissed her again, this time more aggressively. The hot wetness of his tongue prodded her parted lips, only to be stalled momentarily by her tightly clenched teeth. His expert hands wrapped around her back, holding her tighter, nearly squashing her ribs. She felt her knees buckle as the smell of the misty rain permeated his skin, bringing the subtle scent she had noticed earlier to full sexual power.

"Oh, Vanessa," he moaned, his fingers working through her hair, tangling in his firm grasp.

"Michael," she whispered, gasping for breath when he finally released her. Her face glowed warmly in the lamplight as he stared into the green pools the colour of emeralds.

Her eyes widened as if she suddenly realized what was happening. Breaking away from the tickling sensation of his mustache against her upper lip, Vanessa swallowed deeply.

"I can't do this. Michael, I think this has gone too far." The heat in her cheeks burned as she raised a soft hand to touch her face. "I'm sorry. I shouldn't…"

They stood facing each other, oblivious to the looks of passers-by who were forced to step around them on the narrow sidewalk. He traced his fingers along the satiny finish of her jaw, lifting her face toward him again as he whispered. "I wish I could stay another day, get to know you better."

"I wish you could too. Things seem to be moving too fast

for what I'm used to. You have to have patience with me," she said, her green eyes searching his face for hidden clues. Did he really mean what he said, that he wanted to know her better? Or was he just like other men who had pursued her until she refused their advances? She had to control herself, she knew, or she would find herself irresistibly drawn into the situation whether she was ready or not.

"How about visiting me this weekend, at my ranch, no strings attached?" he offered. He held his breath as he watched the surprise reflect on her face.

"I…I'll have to think about it," she whispered, shocked that she allowed the situation to develop this far. Panic rose in her stomach, making her almost dizzy with fear. She started to back away, but he grabbed her wrist and pulled her firmly toward him.

"I'll see you tomorrow, before I leave," he said, the darkened gray of his eyes piercing hers.

"Okay, I'll be at work early anyway. You can drop by before your flight." She hated herself for being so formal with him, but she had to get back on track with the purpose of his visit before her heart ran away with him to the ranch he talked about this afternoon. A chance to ride again, with someone as intriguing as Michael. She hadn't had such an adventuresome weekend in she didn't know how long.

"See you in the morning," he said, bending down to gently kiss her on the forehead. His husky words rang in her ears as she fumbled with the keys for her car. She nodded, unable to speak for fear she would throw herself at this almost total stranger. She was furious with herself for falling for such a man even if he did have an effect on her that she knew she liked. She chastised herself for letting a few glasses of wine make her lose sight of things so easily. What did she need a man in her life for, anyway?

Two

Tears spilled onto her hot cheeks as she pulled into the curved driveway. Vanessa slumped forward on the steering wheel, struggling to switch off the ignition with shaking fingers. Why was she such a fool? Michael had showed interest in her, and she couldn't deny her own feelings of attraction to him, even if she wanted to. Surely he was only feeling the wine as much as she was. She cringed at the memory of his lips on hers. Her blood still ran hot as she forced the image from her mind of what could have happened tonight if she let it.

The rain continued to pelt down, making her move quickly to the doorstep. She fumbled with the lock briefly before almost falling into the doorway. Charlie ran to greet her, his howls of assumed neglect apparent in his voice.

"Oh, Charlie, you thought I'd forgotten you, didn't you?" she asked, picking up the purring ball of orange fur. His nuzzling nose reached under her chin, taking her mind off Michael long enough to carry the cat to the kitchen. She allowed him to jump down onto his favorite chair where his impatience showed no sign of letting up as she fixed his evening meal.

It was just past ten when Vanessa decided to catch up on some reading, trying to escape the thoughts of Michael that kept creeping back into her head. She followed the wooden staircase downstairs ending at the door to the study Mark used for the relaxation he had needed after a busy schedule.

Vanessa pushed open the heavy oak door and peered inside. She rarely entered the room except to dust. For the first three years the thought of seeing Mark sitting behind the immense oak desk made her long for his company in the hours when she couldn't sleep. Now, it was a comforting place to read or think.

She decided to start a fire in the hearth, feeling a bit chilly, matching her mood to the outside weather. There was plenty of kindling and newspaper lining the brass engraved wood box that was placed to one side of the stone fireplace.

It was this room that had sold Mark on the house. Glancing around, she thought it was time to redecorate, surprising herself with the thought, knowing how she vowed to keep his room intact after he died. Perhaps it was time she let go, knowing she needed a more fulfilling life than she had lived in the past four years. She was only thirty, after all. The idea of letting Mark become a part of her past saddened her, but she also felt the burden of guilt being lifted gently from her slender shoulders.

Vanessa poked the blazing fire, threw on another log, and closed the wire screen. She ran her neatly manicured finger along the hardcover selection of books she had bought over the years. Selecting one she hadn't read recently, she pulled it from the shelf and walked slowly toward the comfortable love seat nestled in the bay window. Pulling down the handmade quilt her mother had given her for Christmas two years earlier, she tucked her feet under her and started reading.

It was after midnight when she awoke. The fire had died. The book rested in her lap, open to the page she had started. Slowly she stretched her stiff limbs, pushing herself up off the love seat, wrapping the quilt around her chilly shoulders. The room had cooled off quickly, being an eastern exposure room.

"I'm beat. I'm going to bed, Charlie. See you in the morning," she said as she gently lifted the warm ball that snuggled beside her feet and placed him on the floor. He switched his fluffy tail as he stretched his front legs, back end stuck high in the air.

Walking down the long hallway to the bathroom at the end, she stopped and gingerly raised a finger to touch the cool glass of the collage of pictures of herself and Mark when they were together. She leaned forward to look closer at their innocent faces, taken before they were married. Would she ever be that happy again? It had been four years since his death, and he was the only man she would ever love, she thought, or had Michael already changed that? Would she give him the chance?

Michael, darn him, he kept creeping back into her brain. She unbuttoned her blouse as she walked into the master bedroom. She tossed her clothes on the hope chest beside the door, stripping to nothing before walking into the bathroom to retrieve her silk nightgown. She slipped it over her head, wriggling her slim hips to allow the gown to glide over the curves of her body. She could imagine Michael's hands as he held her tight, not letting her go. Why couldn't she escape the image of Michael, his face glistening in the softly falling rain, as he bent to kiss her? Why did it feel so good? Why did she have to feel so guilty about Mark? She couldn't remember Mark ever making her feel the way Michael could with just one look from those smoky gray eyes.

Her eyes closed as soon as her head nestled against the

plump down pillow, the coolness soothing her fragile nerves.

Falling into a deep sleep, the dream came to her quickly. They were walking along the quiet street again, hand-in-hand this time. The soft, billowing cotton dress she wore grazed her calves as he turned to look deeply into her eyes. Vanessa was aware that the eyes no longer belonged to her beloved Mark, but had changed from light blue to a startling gray colour. He bent to kiss her. Then he suddenly vanished.

She awoke in the morning to the gentle nudging of Charlie, letting her know it was time she let him out. She dragged her feet to the floor, finding her slippers with practiced ease. Charlie ran ahead of her, padding softly down the stairs in his usual fluid movement.

She headed to the bathroom after letting the cat out. Taking one look in the mirror, she groaned. Her eyes were red and puffy from the interrupted sleep. She awoke several times thinking about Michael, dreaming that he had left her alone. The feeling of loss puzzled her, since Michael was only an acquaintance but she couldn't shake the feeling of despair that swept over her. She splashed some cold water on her face, but it didn't help. She tried to focus on things other than Michael, but found it impossible.

Finally Vanessa drew a warm bubble bath. Her shoulders ached, probably from tossing so much last night, trying to avoid any thoughts of Michael Ryan. If she ever saw him again…

She slipped into the frothy warmth, feeling more lost and alone than she could remember. It was almost eight and she wondered if Michael was up. Last night during dinner he said that he had to be in Vancouver this evening, but she wasn't sure what time his flight actually left.

After a good, hot soak, Vanessa felt more like her old self, ready to face the events of the day. What if he meant what he said about the fact that she needed to fulfill her dreams? To do more than just work? She hadn't given her life much thought in the past few years, and she realized that she was afraid to take the chance of becoming emotionally involved again. But worst of all, she was afraid she already was. Vanessa was not the kind to avoid a situation just because she thought it could get unpleasant. She had learned early in business to bite the bullet and face whatever was in her way. She dressed quickly, poured herself a steaming cup of coffee and gulped it down before heading out the door.

He must think me a total idiot, reacting the way I did last night, she thought, as she pulled into her reserved parking spot at the back of the building.

"How did your meeting with Michael go yesterday?" Janice queried as soon as Vanessa entered the office through the back door.

Vanessa was surprised to see her assistant there so early, especially after what happened the day before. She felt suddenly guilty for not calling to check on Janice last night.

Janice had a knack for knowing when something was amiss with her, and she should have seen it coming. Even though they were the best of friends, she hesitated to answer, unsure of her response herself.

"He seemed nice. Good looking, too. So tell me what happened," Janice demanded.

"Promise you won't laugh?"

"I promise."

Vanessa filled her in on the evening, leaving out the reaction to his advances as much as she could without making her friend feel cheated.

"He sounds perfect for you."

"Perfect? When I first saw him, I thought he was gorgeous, but when he spoke, he sounded so...so confident, so sure of himself. I mean, he was so attractive, I think that's what scares me." Vanessa frowned.

"Maybe you dazzled him with your charming smile? Maybe he couldn't resist?" Janice teased.

"He also told me that I was in a good business. Music boxes were for pretty girls. The nerve. I've worked hard for what I've got now, and no man is going to belittle that."

Vanessa was feeling a little indignant, and having an excuse to hate Michael Ryan might make it easier to forget him, she thought.

"Vanessa, if I was in your shoes and a gorgeous…"

"Arrogant…" Vanessa interrupted.

"Intelligent…"

"Presumptuous…" Vanessa countered.

"Presumptuous? How is he presumptuous?" Janice demanded.

"He thought I needed to get a life," Vanessa said, nearly whispering, the hot flush of her cheeks making her feel as if she could glow in the dark.

There was a long silence before Janice responded. "Vanessa, I know how much you and Mark loved each other. It was rough for you then, but that was four years ago. Michael is right. You've got to get on with your life. I hate to see you wither up. It doesn't become you."

Vanessa was shocked. Janice rarely interfered in her personal affairs, although they had confided many things to each other over the past four years.

"Well, I'm not ready for any serious affairs right now," Vanessa said, then turned on her heel, heading for her office. She was unable to see the look of sympathy on her friend's face as Janice slowly shook her head.

After a quick breakfast, Michael headed from the coffee shop to Vanessa's store, which was only a few minutes drive in the rental car he leased from the hotel. The long hours he spent on the incentive program for Vanessa last night paid off. He was finished, but he was tired. He was still angry with himself for advancing on Vanessa like that last night. He planned to apologize first thing when he went to the office with the work. He was pleased with himself for devising what she needed in such a short time.

Straightening the blue silk tie and buttoning the double-breasted navy jacket, Michael hesitated before pulling open the brass-trimmed glass door of The Ballerina Music Box

Company, then stepped inside. He was amazed at the job the cleaning service had done, and he stood for a moment to admire the delicate beauty of the interior of the shop. He cut a striking pose, looming larger than life amid the delicate glass and brass shelving that held the intricate musical novelties.

The soft rap on the glass of her office door brought Vanessa out of her early morning ritual of going over the sales for the day before. Except for the mishap yesterday, business was excellent and she was in better spirits as she looked up from behind the huge oak desk.

Vanessa straightened as Michael's huge form entered the room. She was expecting him this morning, but she was unprepared for the feelings that flitted through her stomach as he advanced toward her, his handsome face clean-shaven and smooth. She had to concentrate hard so as not to rush over to him and stroke the handsome jaw that broke into a smile as he entered the room. The crooked smile showed his pearly white teeth as he greeted her. Vanessa glanced down quickly at the papers in front of her, pretending to straighten up her already neat desk to gain a few valuable moments to collect her thoughts. This was the man who made a move on her last night, and although she had prepared in her head exactly what she wanted to tell him, the words escaped her now.

"Please, have a seat," Vanessa said with as much formality as she could muster, indicating the leather love seat he had reclined on the day before. Her cool words in no way reflected the heat that coursed through her body at the sight of him. She silently cursed her body for betraying her.

"I only have a moment. I thought you would like to see these," he said, refusing the offer to sit as he strode to stand in front of her desk. His eyes pierced hers, holding her entranced as he continued. "I also wanted to apologize for last night. I know I wasn't very gentlemanly, and you didn't deserve such shoddy treatment. I hope this can make up for it." He offered her the single yellow rose he had bought in the flower shop at the hotel. It was wrapped in a delicate cellophane wrapper that crinkled as he handed it to her.

"Oh, Michael, thank you." The surprise was evident in her voice as her shaking hand reached out to pick it up. "You don't have to apologize. Maybe it was my fault, for leading you on. I'm not very good at reading the signals of the opposite sex. I guess you could say I'm very rusty at it." She babbled on, unable to control the flow of nonsense that erupted from her pretty mouth.

Michael smiled again. "I really have to go, so I'll leave these with you. My number is attached to the inside cover. Call me at home Saturday morning if you have any questions. The offer to visit still stands." With a quick nod, he was gone.

Vanessa collapsed into the oversize chair. Now what was she going to do? He had given her his number which clearly indicated the ball was in her court. She knew she wanted to see him again but she didn't think she was prepared to make the next move. She slowly raised the flower to her nose and breathed in its delicate scent.

The flight to Vancouver was the scheduled fifty-five minutes, ending with a smooth landing. Flying was the worst part of his business. He would rather have his feet on the ground or at least be on some sort of ground transportation, but time was money these days, and flying was the way to go.

Michael stooped over to get out of the window seat he had been assigned. His height made it easy to reach the luggage he stowed above. The line moved quickly as the pretty steward-ess bade the passengers good day. Michael hardly noticed the woman as he passed, eager to get to the hotel and settle in and if there was any possible way, he would try to take his mind off Vanessa.

Exiting out of the lower level doors of the Vancouver International Airport, Michael quickly walked to the old Camaro he always kept in the parking lot for his frequent trips to the city. He discovered that it was cheaper than getting around by taxi or renting a car, and having his own transpor-tation allowed him the freedom to travel to any place he wanted when he finished his seminars.

He had been having trouble getting Vanessa off his mind all afternoon. He tried to think about the seminar he was instructing this evening, but was unsuccessful. His mind continued to wander back to the seminar in Prince George, and the woman with the tight black skirt and sexy legs.

He was disappointed he hadn't had more time to talk to Vanessa this morning when he arrived at her store but he could understand why she may not be ready to accept him. Why did he have to be so aggressive? He knew she was different as soon as he saw her, but he still classed her as a woman in a man's world. He had wanted to prove that to her by showing her how he could set up her incentive program for her.

Instead, he dropped it off without any explanation. She was not going to understand all the notes he had entered for her. He checked into his hotel room, and as soon as he was settled, he placed the call. He couldn't wait to return to the ranch the following morning.

Vanessa touched the folder Michael had left lying on her desk. She had opened the file, but resolved not to look at his number in fear she would break down and call it like an anxious schoolgirl who was just given the number of a popular boy. But that was being silly, she knew, because he was now on a plane to Vancouver. It would be tomorrow before he arrived home. She opened the file gingerly with one hand, the other holding her second coffee of the morning. Taking a quick sip of the hot black liquid, she glanced at the notes jotted along the side of the page. There was a handwritten page at the end, outlining all the recommendations Michael felt she needed to make her program successful.

She looked closely at the figures he had used. He certainly went over the file carefully, she noticed. There were a few questions she felt she wanted to ask him. Glancing at his card, she made a note of when he said to call. The number was scrawled on the front of his business card. Probably his ranch number, she thought, setting it in the corner of her blotter. Should she call? What was she going to say? He had invited her to the ranch, but he didn't give her a chance to accept or decline. Maybe he was as nervous as she was about their relationship.

Her phone jangled loudly, pulling her out of her reverie. "Yes, Janice?" she said, answering the blinking button that was her outside call line.

"How are you?" the deep, familiar voice came over the wire.

Vanessa felt the sudden surge of blood pulse through her veins. Her voice cracked in her suddenly dry throat.

"Fine."

It was silent for a long moment. Vanessa waited for him to explain why he called.

"Did you get a chance to go over the file?" he asked.

"I found the notes you wrote…"

"I wanted to talk to you about them. I didn't have time this morning, so…"

"I know. And yes, I did. You spent a lot of time on them. I was impressed."

"Good. Bring the file with you, that is, if you have decided to take me up on my offer. I'll be home for the next week, then I fly to Vancouver again. The time away from work will do you some good, and I could spend some time in the great outdoors. I have this little place in Blue River I was telling you about. I know you would like the break." He hoped he was convincing her because all it sounded like was nervous prattle, which he knew it was. He desperately wanted to see her again, and the ache in his lower body was testament to that.

Vanessa straightened up, not realizing she was holding her breath until she spoke. His slow, sexy undertone sent shivers down her back. "I…I'd love to. Can you give me some directions?"

He quickly obliged, as Vanessa scribbled on the closest piece of paper she could find.

"Be sure to bring some riding clothes." He paused. Then softly he said, "I can't wait to see you again."

"Yes, see you tomorrow sometime," she said, heart still

hammering at the sound of his husky voice.

Vanessa replaced the receiver and fell back in her chair, her heart thumping wildly. She was going to have to pack and get a good night's sleep, and arrange for Janice to feed Charlie, and, what else? Her mind raced with the mounting excitement about taking a chance on new love, if that is what it was going to be. She knew she would have a hard time refusing him anything he wanted. Unsure if she could curb the unfulfilled need that arose in her every time the thought of being near him crossed her mind, Vanessa decided she would have to take things slowly and resolved to watch herself until she could figure his motives.

After finishing up what she was working on, Vanessa gathered her coat and purse and locked her door behind her. Janice looked up from the typing she was doing.

"What's up?" she asked, noticing the distracted look on her boss's face.

"Oh, I'm going to take a vacation from this place. And I'm putting you in charge, okay?" She felt brown eyes penetrating the back of her head as she leafed through the morning's mail Janice was about to sort.

"A vacation?" The shock in Janice's voice was evident. "You haven't had a vacation in four years. What's the sudden plan all about now, Vanessa?"

"Well, if you must know, I'm going to spend a few days on Michael Ryan's ranch. The fresh air will do me good," she added, blushing furiously.

"That's not all that will do you good," Janice teased.

"That's enough," Vanessa said, holding back a case of giggles.

"If you say so, boss, but let me tell you, if I had a chance to spend some time with a gorgeous hunk of man...well, I'd make sure it was well spent if you know what I mean. You sure could use it," Janice spluttered.

Vanessa laughed. "Is it so obvious? I guess you can read me better than I can read myself. He just called, from the hotel in Vancouver, and I've decided to take him up on his invitation to spend some time on his ranch. He said 'no strings attached' so I should be safe enough, shouldn't I?" she asked, suddenly feeling a little apprehensive at the thought of going to a strange place alone.

"Have a good time. And Vanessa, don't worry about us here. We'll get along just fine without you."

"That's another thing I'm afraid of," she said as she was about to waltz out the door, her mind on the things she'd need to get before she could leave in the morning. She turned to look at her friend once more. "And wipe that silly grin off your face. I never said we are going to do what you're thinking."

"I never thought what you think I was thinking," Janice said, laughing at her friend's embarrassment.

"Oh, you're impossible."

Janice nodded, trying to make a somber face, but failed.

"I have a bit of running around to do, and then I'll be back around ten. See you later," Vanessa said, scurrying out the front door.

Janice returned to her desk and picked up the phone. She dialed the number, spoke quickly, and hung up. Half an hour later the huge bouquet of bright orange tiger lilies arrived just a few minutes after Vanessa returned.

"What's this?" Vanessa asked, eyes wide in amazement, as she watched the twenty or so beautiful stalks of tiger lilies seemingly walk into the room with a pair of legs attached to the bottom of the pot.

The delivery boy set them on her desk as instructed by Janice, and made a hasty retreat.

Vanessa picked the orange envelope out of the arrangement, and opened it precariously.

"Go get 'em, tiger. J."

"All right, I will," Vanessa said to herself as she picked up the briefcase packed full of reports she intended to take with her to work on in the evenings.

Janice was conspicuously absent from her desk when Vanessa left. Seeing the note pad turned in her direction, Vanessa quickly grabbed a pen and wrote, "Your turn will come, and I will be there to owe you one. V." With that she left, an excitement she hadn't felt in years mounting inside her.

After a short afternoon of shopping for boots and new lingerie, Vanessa headed home. Charlie greeted Vanessa with his usual howl and rubbed against her legs. Bending down, she gently stroked the long hair, allowing the cat to nuzzle her knee with his head butt.

"I suppose you are just starving, aren't you, Charlie?" she asked. He was hot on her heels as he followed her into the kitchen. As she placed the dirty dishes that she had left lying around the night before in the sink, she leaned against the counter, watching the neighbors' children play in the back-yard. She had watched the two children grow from toddlers to school age, but for the last four years she hadn't kept in touch with their activities as much as when she stayed home. They still said hello to her when their paths crossed.

She pushed herself away from the window, trying not to think about the family she and Mark never had. Vanessa had hoped to have two children of her own, to love and take care of. When they discovered it was Mark who couldn't have children, they were talking about adopting. That was before— now... Vanessa shook her head slowly. She was thirty now, time to reconsider what life held for her. She was told she would stand an excellent chance of adopting a child even though she would be a single parent, but it wasn't quite the way she wanted it. The cozy kitchen felt suddenly empty of warmth. Vanessa glanced out the window above the sink, her thoughts far from the dreary rain that pelted softly against the glass.

Vanessa prepared herself a lasagna dinner, popping the frozen dish into the microwave. Cooking for one had become a challenge for her and she always had a well-balanced meal waiting when she got home from the office. Most of her Sundays were spent making things she loved, experimenting with new recipes, and freezing them into single portions. It did get a little lonely with no one to talk to though.

After packing her suitcase and overnight bag, Vanessa retired to bed, exhausted but elated. The excitement mounted in her as she tossed in bed, unable to stop her racing mind from traveling to Blue River before her.

Three

The warmth of the Saturday morning sun glinting through the peach-coloured venetian blind gently caressed Vanessa's smooth, exposed shoulder. Rolling over, she glanced at the clock. It was well past seven, and the aroma of fresh-brewed coffee floated up the stairs. She silently thanked the coffee-maker industry for programmable coffee-makers. Leisurely, she stretched her long arms over her head, then tossed the coverlet across the bed. Vanessa grabbed her peach velour housecoat and wrapped it tightly around her slim middle.

The bright kitchen welcomed her. The smell of coffee was enticing as she poured herself a cup in her favorite earthenware mug. She smiled, remembering the time Mark had presented her with the mug, hand-painted with a picture of a ballerina on it. The heaviness of the cup seemed to upset the delicate balance of the tiny figure painted on it. But she had loved it anyway.

Vanessa had spent the evening thinking about Michael's offer, unsure if she was ready for a relationship, if that was what it was going to be.

She was having second thoughts and was considering calling Michael first thing this morning and bowing out. There did not have to be any strings attached, she consoled herself, even if he did work on the incentive program for her. He had done it of his own free will. She at least owed him a personal thank-you, she finally decided as she gathered up her bags and headed out to her car.

Traffic was heavy on the Hart Highway north of the city early Saturday morning. Vanessa was caught in the pulp mill shift change traffic before she realized what she had done. If she'd left just fifteen minutes earlier, or five minutes later, it would only take her ten minutes to get out of the city. Now it would be almost twenty. Silently she chastised herself for having that second cup of coffee but she felt she needed it to summon up all the courage she could muster to make the trip.

He surveyed the neat, white and blue kitchen that had been his grandmother's favorite place. Vanessa would be here in less than six hours, and he had a few things to take care of before then. He wanted her stay to be enjoyable. He could use a bit of relaxation on the ten-acre ranch himself after his busy schedule the past few weeks.

Michael pulled on the black cowboy boots he left sitting on the mat by the screen door. The fresh spring breeze wafted up from the front lawn. Les, his only hired hand, was just completing cutting the grass on the ride-on lawnmower when Michael peered out the door.

Reaching for the dirt-streaked felt stetson he used for doing chores, Michael tried to keep focused on the work at hand. It was a tough task considering he never was the kind to dwell on a woman. But he sened that Vanessa was different.

The last two days had played havoc on his usually methodical brain. During his last seminar, he found he had to keep totally focused on what he was doing, or his mind would wander back to her.

Planting the dusty hat on his head, he sauntered over to Les. "Ready to go?" Michael asked.

Les turned his tanned, weather-lined face, shining in the morning heat. "Yep. You shore you won't be needin' me for the next little while?" he asked, rubbing his forehead with the bandanna he kept tied around his wrinkled neck. Michael had known Les ever since the day he came to live with his grandparents on the ranch, almost twenty-five years ago. After his grandparents passed away, Michael and Les mutually agreed that Les would have the original house on the hill if he wished to stay and work on the ranch.

"No, I'm sure I'll manage. Anyway, your granddaughter has been waiting to see you for a while now. I'm feeling guilty enough for keeping you here so much. I really appreciate your help, you know." Michael patted the old-timer on the shoulder. They turned and headed to Les' place to gather the hand's luggage. "Anyway, most of the work is caught up around here. What do you think?" Michael asked.

"I think you're tryin' to git rid of me," Les teased. He could still make Michael feel like a schoolboy, shy about bringing a girlfriend home, knowing the teasing he would get.

"Right, Les," he said, slightly embarrassed, but jokingly. "I need you out of my hair for the week."

"I can take a hint. Want me to pick this lady friend of yours up?" he asked. "Maybe she'd fall for me, and you wouldn't have to put up with the intrusion on your privacy." Les grinned at Michael, obviously enjoying seeing Michael squirm.

"Cut it out, Les." Michael's tanned face glowed warmly in the midmorning sunshine. Both were over six feet tall, but the elder had a decided stoop to his shoulders from years of riding the range and hard work. They reached the front steps where Michael found the suitcases already neatly stacked against the porch door. "That's all?" Michael asked, watching Les as he dug the keys out of his trouser pants. Les' shaking fingers locked the door as Michael thought how he was going to miss the old guy when he was gone. Michael cared for the old man, knowing how lonely he was for his only family.

Les grinned at the younger man. "Don't need much at my age. Not like when you flit off to the big city with your laptop 'n all."

"Listen, old-timer, I could replace you in a second," Michael tossed back.

"Sure, but you'll never git anyone as charmin' as me, now, will ya?"

Michael gave a hearty laugh, but inside his heart wrenched at the thought of losing Les. The old fellow was nearing eighty. Sometimes Michael worried about leaving him alone but Les would have nothing of a babysitter around at his age, he would tell him.

"Becky's bin talkin' 'bout me stayin' on with her for the past while. I can't seem to git it through her perdy little head that I'm doin' fine here. She bribes me with the excuse that I'll have more time for Adam. Ya know, he's almost seven now. I don't know where the time has gone. The two of them are doin' fine, she says, but sometimes I worry about her. Vancouver is a big place for a country girl," he said.

"Well, if you want, I can arrange for someone to look after the place while I'm away. You can stay for as long a visit as you'd like with them, Les. That Douglas boy down the road has been at me to look after the place ever since last summer when he got his license. We could try that, if you like." Michael didn't want Les to feel obliged to stay. He had noticed lately how much slower Les was moving, although Les rarely complained of the arthritis that bothered his joints, especially in the rainy spring.

"I'll talk to her about it and let ya know."

They drove to town in silence, each consumed with his own thoughts of the next few days. Michael wondered if he had everything Vanessa might want for her short visit.

The drive from Prince George to Blue River was shorter than Vanessa expected as she cruised along the paved highway, passing the increasingly mountainous terrain before turning at the Tete Jaune junction to take Highway 5 south through the serenity of the Columbia Mountain range.

The four hours she spent alone in the car seemed to take forever as her mind wallowed in the thoughts that there were underlying reasons for her agreeing to this vacation. Janice insinuated something Vanessa wasn't quite prepared for, although she put up a good front about it. She could talk to Janice whenever she needed to, but only to a certain level before she hid her feelings.

Maybe I need a therapist, she mused, glancing in the rearview mirror. A yellow Jeep was gaining on her faster than she would have liked. The shadowy figure behind the wheel was waving his right arm in the direction of the ditch. She stepped on it, not prepared to be pulled over on a lonely stretch by a stranger.

Unwanted thoughts of the Wells Gray Park murders of a few years back prodded her brain. Suddenly she realized just how vulnerable she was, traveling on a quiet highway through the middle of nowhere. The Jeep started to honk. Vanessa's pulse raced. Green eyes wide, she glanced behind her in the mirror, considering her options.

Vanessa decided to slow down, only because she knew the turn off to Michael's ranch was not far away and she didn't want to miss it and be stuck with the lunatic on the road behind her.

In her panic, Vanessa misjudged the grade of the hill she was slowly climbing. The yellow Jeep overtook her halfway up and slowed down itself. Vanessa backed off only to find the signal light of the Jeep flashing excitedly. The vehicle ahead of her turned into the same road she had calculated to be the ranch. She approached slowly, wary of being alone on the road with this maniac. She hadn't been passed either way by any traffic for the last hour of her journey.

As she slowed, she took a second glance at the tall, tanned

cowboy, hat now placed strategically on his head, not allowing her to see the shadowed eyes that watched her pull her car
to a stop.

She wondered how she was going to maneuver the vehicle
around the Jeep as he sauntered over to her. She tried to tell
herself to settle down, not to be childishly frightened in broad
daylight. Nothing was going to happen to her, she consoled
herself, but her stomach clenched uncontrollably. She rolled
the window down cautiously as the checkered shirt was
replaced by tanned arms settling themselves folded across her
open window.

"Michael Ryan," she exclaimed, pushing him back as she
flung open the door, knocking him slightly off balance. "You
had me half-scared out of my wits." Her green eyes flashed in
the sunlight as she jumped out of the tiny red sports car.

He started to laugh as he turned and headed for his Jeep,
leaving her standing by her car door with her mouth open.

She stormed over the short distance of rocky road to his
vehicle.

Vanessa watched as he leaned over the black leather of the
driver's seat. He was obviously trying to retrieve something in
the back seat. Her anger was distracted momentarily as her
eyes ran the length of his long legs, muscles stretching to the
limit, nearly bursting the seams as he strained forward. The
rear view isn't bad, she thought, stepping back for a better
look.

Michael glanced back at that instant, catching her in a
stance he would expect to find someone who was viewing a
work of art in a museum. One arm folded across her small
chest held the elbow of the other. The hand held a delicate
chin, tilted slightly to one side. A bemused smile played on the
creamy-skinned face. But the most breath-taking feature had
to be her eyes. They shone like emeralds in the bright sunlight.
He banged his head as he emerged, rubbing the spot that
appeared as his hat toppled to the ground.

Vanessa tried to suppress the laughter. The annoyance she
felt a moment ago was gone as he turned, hand still on his head,

the other behind his back. She hardly had time to realize he was hiding something when he presented her with a bouquet of wild flowers, mostly daisies and tiger lilies.

"So you think you can soften me up with flowers, do you?" she asked, her voice slightly unsteady. Having finally arrived and seeing him in the flesh again, she felt a nervous flutter in her stomach. Her heart pounded as he took his hand from his head and slid it behind her waist in one swift motion.

"I picked them especially for you," he said. He brushed her lips with his, testing the waters with his soft caress. He held her tighter so she couldn't run from him this time.

Vanessa returned his tentative kiss, but with more passion than he had shown, surprising them both. She reveled in the feel of his powerful arms enveloping her. "Michael," she whispered. All the feeling she was denying existed, rose to the surface, making her instantly melt in his powerful embrace.

"Sorry," he said, releasing his grasp on her slim waist. "It's just so good to see you. I had thoughts of you changing your mind at the last minute." He flashed a handsome smile at her before guiding her back to her car.

"Come on, I'll lead you in. The road is narrow and you certainly would wreck that thing," he said, pointing to her vehicle, "if you kept up the pace you seemed so comfortable with." He vanished into the Jeep before she could explain.

A sudden, uncontrollable fear shot through him, a fear that she would not like what he had to offer her here. She was a sophisticated lady, he thought, a worried frown hidden under the felt hat he had replaced on his head after the brief embrace.

After parking his Jeep in front of the house, Michael jumped out and hurried over to the little sports car, opening the door for Vanessa almost before she killed the engine. "I'll show you to your room so you can freshen up," he said. He took her keys and quickly retrieved her bags from the trunk of her car while she stood taking in the sights of the place she tried to picture in her mind the last few days. She had never done it justice, she realized, as she took in the fresh coat of white paint that covered the front of the Victorian style farmhouse. The gabled windows overlooked an expanse of land dappled with two barns, a shed, garage, and tiny guest house off to one side. The corral contained two beautiful horses, and her blood raced at the thought of being able to ride again. She grabbed the flowers off the dash before joining Michael.

"I hope you like it," Michael said as he held open the door to the warm kitchen. The aroma of a roast in the oven assailed her nostrils as she stepped inside, flowers still held tightly in her delicate hand. The room was bright and cozy, neatly decorated in blue and white. The lace curtains added a uniquely feminine touch to the kitchen, instantly making her wary of the possible existence of a woman other than the grandmother he talked about.

"I live alone," he said, as if reading her mind. He opened the door to the oven to check on the roast. "Unless you count Les."

"Les?" she asked, arching a golden eyebrow as she tried to hide the jealous feelings she was puzzled to find she carried.

"Yeah, he stayed on with the ranch when my grandparents died. I guess you could say I inherited him. He's a great old guy. He's gone to Vancouver to visit his granddaughter for a couple of weeks, so we're alone now."

Vanessa swallowed. She knew she hadn't thought through all the possibilities of going to a place with a man she hardly knew. She hadn't wanted to give it much thought, she decided, knowing the more rational side of her would have forbid her to come.

"Here, I'll show you your room now." Vanessa followed him silently up the hardwood stairs. "It used to be my grandmother's. I hope you like it," he said, holding the wooden door open for her as she moved around him, peering into the most feminine room she had ever seen.

"It's gorgeous," she said, stepping softly inside. The room was filled with touches of femininity. The lace curtains were neatly held back with faded yellow satin ribbons, framing the window. The warmth of the room reflected the heat in her body as she realized just how close he stood behind her, his breath gently caressing her neck. She turned to face him, unsure of what to do next.

"There's a bathroom at the end of the hall." He pointed. His eyes held hers a moment longer before he reluctantly removed himself from her room. The thought of Vanessa entwined in his arms brought back the familiar stirring in his loins which he felt more frequently now. It frustrated him, being as unable to control his reactions to her as a schoolboy on his first date.

"Thanks," she murmured to his retreating back, then turned to relax in the quiet solitude that emanated from the papered walls. She flopped down on the big four-poster bed and looked out the window, as he left the room.

The bed squeaked and groaned with old age, and Vanessa wondered how it would protest under the weight of two people. She felt her face grow hot as she rolled over onto her stomach to get a better view of the front yard where the vehicles were parked. Vanessa closed her eyes. Seeing him again, tall, tanned and sexy in his tight-fitting jeans caused Vanessa more than a few moments of idle day-dreaming about the two of them intimate on the squeaky old bed.

The faint tingle remained on her lips from his kiss. She raised her hand to cover her mouth, pressing softly. It had been so long since she had been kissed by a man, not counting the surprise attack she encountered just a few days before with Michael.

A soft tapping sounded from the half-opened door interrupted her peaceful thoughts. Michael stepped back inside the cozy room.

"It'll be about ten minutes before supper is ready," he said, his voice low, almost a whisper.

"Great," she said, jumping up from her reclining position. She was embarrassed by the sudden squeaking sound, wondering if Michael thought the same thoughts about how tempting it would be to make the bed squeak on purpose. "I'll just freshen up a bit and be right down," she said, moving to retrieve her bags.

"Enjoy yourself. It's your vacation. I'll give a shout when it's time to eat." His eyes lingered on her breasts, making her nipples respond under the thin blouse she wore. His scrutiny made her shiver inwardly, holding her in a frozen stance until his eyes released her as he turned to finish with the business of making dinner.

Vanessa settled on the bed for a moment, slowly rotating her stiff shoulders while she took in more of the delicate surroundings. The room was perfect for her, she thought, with the feminine touches of lace and ribbon on the curtains. Even the antique dresser was lined with delicately scented paper. On the vanity desk, pressed against one wall, sat a beautifully carved jewelry box. Vanessa wandered over to it and opened it up only to discover it was a music box. She snapped the lid shut immediately, hoping the sounds could not be heard in the kitchen. She didn't want him to think she was snooping, but the curiosity about the delicately carved box intrigued her. Her heart ached as she remembered Mark had never given her one, even though his company sold thousands annually.

She walked back to the bed, suddenly realizing she had left her bouquet on the dresser and looked around the room for a vase to set them in. The only suitable container was a ceramic pitcher and basin set, which was displayed on the dresser. She carried the pitcher to the bathroom to fill it.

The bathroom was tastefully decorated in cedar and brass, much like her own at home, she realized. She wondered if Michael or his grandmother had remodeled this room.

Returning to the guest room, she placed the pitcher in its basin. Lifting the flowers to her face, she took a deep breath of the sweet scent. The bouquet held mostly daisies but it was tastefully arranged with a few wild purple flowers as well as three tiger lilies. She thought with remorse of the ones she left to wilt in the office then decided Janice would take care of them in her absence.

She gathered her make up bag and headed into the bathroom to freshen up. She remembered Janice's card with the "Go get 'em, tiger" written on it. It seemed to her that it didn't take much for her to do just that. Something about Michael Ryan made it that way, she thought, as she closed the bathroom door gently behind her.

Michael busied himself making the remainder of the meal he had planned earlier that morning. The sound of the water running upstairs brought back memories of earlier days when he didn't live alone. It felt good to have a visitor around, especially such an attractive one. He whistled softly as he finished preparing the vegetables, putting them into appropriate pots on the stove. He was fortunate to have learned how to cook from his grandmother, because he was sure he would have starved if he hadn't. He actually enjoyed cooking, trying new things.

Michael heard the taps being turned off as he finished wiping the countertop. He was anxious that Vanessa like the place, and annoyed at himself for thinking about it. Wasn't he only letting himself in for another heartbreak when he found that she was just another city girl who would get bored with the country life? Could he take the chance on her? On love?

After she had finished changing into a natural cotton shirt, tied at the waist, and her best pair of form-fitting jeans, she headed down the narrow stairs toward the kitchen. For thirty, she still had the body of a twenty-year-old, Janice always told her.

She watched with interest as Michael set the table with fine china and silverware. He was unaware of her presence until she spoke.

"Can I help with anything?"

He turned, his broad shoulders blocking the remaining sunlight that filtered through the window above the sink.

"No, I've got it all under control. Can I offer you a drink? A glass of wine, perhaps?" he said, reaching for the chilled white wine he had purposefully placed in the fridge earlier.

"That sounds great." She raised her head, sniffing the air. "It smells terrific in here," she said, walking across the expansive kitchen to accept the glass.

He poured himself one as well and raised it in a silent toast. She did the same, meeting his eyes as she took her first sip. The wine was light, and slightly bubbly, the kind she had during their dinner, she recalled.

He motioned for her to take a seat while he stood at the island expertly carving the roast. The gravy bubbled on the stove, and he gave it a quick stir. Vanessa watched, fascinated, as he handled the meal with ease.

"Do you have any brothers or sisters?" he asked, cheerfully, as he placed the cooling roast on the table.

"I have a twin sister. She's married, with two children. She lives in Edmonton so I don't see her too often."

"It must be fun having a twin," Michael said, turning his attention from the stove to her, imagining what two of these lovely blondes would look like together.

"Sometimes," Vanessa said, "but there are times when it's tough, too." She didn't want to get into a deep conversation on the pros and cons of having a twin, even though she knew that most people found it a fascinating topic.

"How's that?" he asked, not allowing her to escape the discussion. As long as he kept her talking and his hands busy, he knew he could keep from dropping everything to scoop her up in his arms and carry her off to the seclusion of his bedroom. The thought of doing just that played havoc on his hormones even as he spoke.

"Well, you're never really your own person, or at least that's what I found when I was growing up. We used to dress the same. We even sound the same over the phone. We have the same laugh. Things like that. I guess it's harder to be an individual when you have someone that looks just like you."

"I wouldn't know what that was like. I was an only child." Michael continued to watch her over the rim of his wine glass, taking only a few seconds to stir the gravy, before continuing to concentrate on her.

"Being an only child has its pros and cons, too, doesn't it?" she asked.

"I guess it does. But sometimes I wish I had an older

brother or sister. My grandmother was very good to me, but I know I missed a lot by not having a family around," he added, catching her shining green eyes staring at him.

"I never told anyone this, but Gram was the best thing that ever happened to me. She was the one who always worked on smoothing the edges on me; at least, that's what she always said."

"Her work paid off," Vanessa said quietly before she could stop herself.

Michael looked up, silently acknowledging the compliment with shining gray eyes. He held Vanessa's gaze a second longer, fighting to control the urge to toss aside the meal and devour her instead. What is wrong with me, he thought, as he visibly shook his head before bending back to cut the roast.

"Tell me about the ranch, why it keeps you here even though you seem to suit the city life," she said, changing the subject. Her eyes followed his every move, watching him as he lowered his broad shoulders to place the last of the meal in front of her before taking his seat across from her. Vanessa felt the heat rise in her, his nearness enveloping her like an electric blanket on a cold winter night.

Michael lifted the wine bottle, noting it was already half emptied before topping up each of their glasses. "I inherited the ranch from my grandparents, as you know, but I was also raised by them since I was twelve." Vanessa nodded, waiting for him to continue as they helped themselves to the delicious meal. His eyes met hers as he looked up to offer her a dish.

"It was hard that first summer, losing my parents and all, but I soon learned to love it here. I knew this is where I wanted to stay. The mountains, the trails, the horses. It was a perfect place for a difficult youngster. My grandmother taught me so much about life, and love," he added, catching her blush at the last statement.

"She sounds like a remarkable woman. I think I would have liked to have met her." Vanessa took a mouthful of potatoes smothered in gravy. "Umm, good," she mumbled, impressed that he actually could cook.

"She was." He stared at her over his glass as he raised it to his lips. Her eyes sparkled in the soft glow of the evening light filtering through the kitchen window. Michael purposefully dimmed the overhead light in an effort to set the mood for his plans for the evening. He wasn't sure she would be as receptive as he imagined, but he was determined to win her over.

Vanessa shifted uneasily in her chair. Somehow this fine specimen sitting across from her made her feel more feminine than she had in a long time, even though she wore a plain blouse and jeans, which she suddenly regretted putting on. His eyes bore into hers as she took another sip of the wine. She had better cool it with the wine if she was going to keep her wits about her. She reminded herself she was alone with an almost total stranger. What was she doing here anyway?

"You haven't told me very much about yourself, Vanessa."

"What do you want to know?" she asked, placing her glass beside her empty plate. She didn't realize she was so hungry and it was past seven already. Now, the nearness of the night made for a more intimate setting than she had imagined.

"All about you." His gaze held her, the glittering silver of his eyes making her blood rush through her veins, warming parts of her she thought would never be alive again. She blushed at his intent stare, thankful for the dimness of the room.

"You already know about me. I own…"

"I know, I know, a music box company," he interrupted. "I want to know the real you. How did a woman as beautiful as you not remarry?" He was curious, and very straightforward.

"First, I'm no beauty…"

"'Beauty is in the eye of the beholder.' Isn't that how it goes?" he said. "And you are beautiful, whether you want to admit it or not." His statement hung in the glow of the candle he had placed in the center of the table just before they started their dinner.

Vanessa chose not to argue with him. Her feelings of

inadequacy about how she stacked up against her sister were not his problem. She answered his question with all the aplomb she could muster. "Well, I guess the right man never came along." She rested her chin on her folded hands, elbows on the table.

"What if he did?" Michael held his breath, watching her intently. Where did he ever get such ideas, he wondered. He thought he wasn't the marrying kind, but something about this woman brought out the instinct to protect and shelter this adorable creature. Maybe he changed somewhere along the way, but he could not place where or when.

"I'll have to wait and see, won't I?" she said flippantly. The conversation was making her uneasy. She thought she had had everything when Mark was alive, but now, after four lonely years, she knew she needed the strength and love a man could give her. She knew deep down that it was this man, but she was afraid to let herself in for any more hurt in her life. She quickly changed the subject as she started to clear the table.

"Sit down. I'll get that," he said, taking the dish out of her hand, but not before he moved his arm across her forearm to remove the plate. The coarseness of the hair on his arm grazed her soft, bare arm, making her skin tingle electrically for a moment as he walked to the sink. "I can finish these later. How about a drink on the verandah?" he offered.

"Another wine would be fine." Vanessa was hesitant to make the evening pass too quickly, feeling slightly anxious about being alone overnight, now that the time was near. She decided the wine would help her bolster her courage to answer his underlying questions honestly. She felt he wanted her for his own, and it scared her. Was she actually ready for a relationship? Is that why she agreed to visit? Vanessa watched the muscles in his broad back flex as he set the dishes down. She couldn't take her eyes off his attractive physique. She wanted to walk over to him and wrap her arms around his tight waist. She stood up.

As if reading her mind, he stalked over to her, poured the last of the wine into the glass she held out to him, and placed his arm around her waist. He guided her silently to the front verandah, gently supporting her weaving body against his.

"I think I might have already had enough to drink," she said, suddenly remembering the dinner they had enjoyed together in Prince George, and the moments that followed it as they danced together in the intimacy of the lounge.

She tripped over the mat inside the door. If he hadn't had such a good hold on her, she would have fallen onto the wooden decking. Michael swooped her up into his powerful arms just as she faltered. She nearly spilled her wine on both of them.

Michael lowered her onto the front porch swing, set his glass on the railing, then walked to the other end of the porch to retrieve the white painted table to place in front of them. She closed her eyes briefly, feeling as if she had been transported to another time, another era, where things went slower, where time was not important.

Her glass was almost to her full lips when she saw it coming, full bore, across the lawn. She gasped, searching for air that would not enter her lungs. She was six again, helpless against the weight of the lunging beast that trapped her beneath it. The huge animal pounced on her, paws dirtying her light blouse above her breasts. She braced herself, unable to scream as the full-grown German shepherd sniffed her face and hair, trapping her under his weight. The wine spilled down her chin, dribbled onto her blouse, mixing with the overpowering smell of wet mutt.

"Major, get down," Michael commanded, hauling the overly-friendly beast off his guest. "Vanessa, are you okay? Bad dog." He lifted the dog off by sheer force on its collar. Major sulked over to the corner, head hung low but still keeping an eye on the unexpected company.

The dog had been sleeping in the barn, protecting his livestock, as he always did when Michael was away or a strange vehicle arrived. Michael stared at the shrinking body sitting in the swing. "Are you all right?" he asked, placing his hand comfortingly on her pale forehead.

"I…I'm just…I…" Vanessa could no longer hold back the tears. She sobbed uncontrollably, hunching over, her feet brought up under her, curling herself into a little ball as if she were a child. Michael sat down beside her, pulling her close, worry clouding his gray eyes.

"It's okay. It's okay." He rocked her back and forth on the swing, holding her until the tears finally subsided, and the shaking ceased.

Vanessa wiped the tears from her dirt-streaked face, pushing the wisps of bangs out of her eyes, trying to cover the fear she always had of large dogs. Embarrassment turned to outrage as she jumped to her feet.

"How could you? How could you let that beast jump all over me like that?" She was trembling visibly, unable to stop the shakiness from surfacing.

"I said I was sorry. He got away. He doesn't normally jump on people." Michael shrugged his huge shoulders before rising to tower over her. "You must have a cat," he surmised.

"A cat? Well, yes, I do, but what has that got to do with it?" She jutted her chin up to him, pouting furiously.

Michael tilted his head back and laughed loudly. Vanessa glared at him. He had no right to laugh at her. She turned to push her way around him, anxious to head into the house to change her clothes. The thought of packing up and leaving was not far from her mind.

"Major loves cats. He must smell yours on you, although what I smell is something a little more provocative than cat," he teased, trying to erase her dark mood. Michael grabbed her arm as she tried to squeeze past. He pulled her up close to him, his hard torso pressing into her soft contours. He moved his taut leg between hers as he edged her back against the roughness of the shingled wall.

Vanessa tingled involuntarily, struggling to contain the warm sensation that was beginning to pool just below her stomach. His hands still held her wrists, making it impossible to struggle. What scared her was the fact that she didn't want to struggle, didn't want to be free of his overpowering presence. Her eyes widened as she realized what she could be getting into. With a quick shove, she set him back enough to duck under his arm and head into the house on a fast run.

"Vanessa, wait, I'm sorry," he said, chasing her inside as she ran for the stairs. Her heart pounded as she raced for the safety of her room, the only place she could escape the charging hulk behind her.

Michael landed his full weight on her at the top of the stairs, tackling her, pulling her to the floor where she twisted and squirmed, shouting at him at the top of her lungs. She fought him with all her strength, banging her elbow on the table in the hallway, as he laughed at her feeble efforts to escape his mighty grasp.

The weight of his warm body pressed her back hard against the wooden floor, trapping her, making it impossible to battle his advances. She felt the soft wetness of his mouth as it explored the tender flesh of her neck, moving across her cheek, settling on her lips.

He kissed her hard on the mouth, squelching the curses flowing from her dainty lips. She moved her head to the side, desperate to yell out, but realizing too late that no one would hear her. He prodded her teeth apart with his strong tongue, probing deeply as she returned the kiss. Her hands, no longer pinned beside her, ran long, graceful fingers through his thick mass of hair, holding him to her as all the passion pent up in her exploded inside.

She caught her breath long enough to call his name again.

"Michael. Michael, stop it." She was breathless and flushed with wanting him.

He raised himself off her, rolling onto the hardwood floor, still draping his arm across her ribs, holding her down. She didn't struggle, but her eyes were wide in surprise. He smiled at her.

"You can't deny the attraction we have to one another, can you?" he asked, his smoky eyes penetrating her wide, green ones.

Vanessa gulped hard before she answered. "I know I'm

attracted to you. That's what scares me," she whispered. "I'm not used to this," she added, raising her hand to lightly touch his cheek, running her finger along his mustache before he captured it in his mouth.

"Umm, you taste good," he murmured, then lifted his arm off her warm body. "That was fun," he said, laughing softly. "Want to try it again?"

"Michael Ryan, I did not come her to be molested. I accepted your offer of a quiet retreat because that is what I thought it would be." She smoothed the few loose tresses that fell around her long neck, come loose from the French braid she still wore. She perched on one elbow, still lying on the hard floor. He no longer held her but she dared not move until they settled this.

He watched her through gray eyes that shone with barely concealed anger. "What else should I think, when you accepted? If you were in my place, wouldn't you get the same impression?" he asked, incredulous that she could play the innocent victim so well.

Her soft green eyes misted as she held back the tears that threatened to spill over. How could he have thought she came down for an affair? They never even discussed the possibility. The hurt expression showed in her face as she said softly, "I'll go get packed now. You obviously don't want me here, at least not for the same reason I came." She crouched onto bended knees as he grabbed her arm.

"Wait. I'm sorry. I should have known you wouldn't be like that. I don't know what came over me."

She gazed into the sad gray eyes. Michael offered his hand to pull her to her feet. "Please stay. I promise not to do anything you don't want me to. Deal?"

She grappled with the idea of packing up now, knowing intuitively that she was going to have a very difficult time keeping her own passions under control, let alone watching out for his. If there was going to be something between them, she wanted it to be because she said so. "Deal," she whispered, admitting to herself that she wasn't prepared to leave yet. She knew she wanted him as much as he seemed to want her, and she only needed time to adjust. She accepted the outstretched hand, rough as it was, but gentle as well. She wondered why she reacted to his touch so vehemently when she knew how his advances made her feel alive again. This was just going to take a little more time, that's all, she convinced herself.

"Goodnight," she said, his hand still holding hers for a moment longer. She closed her bedroom door behind her, wrapping her arms tightly around her chest as she tried to calm the shaking. After her heart rate returned to a more normal pace, she changed into the nightie she had brought. Her face was still hot from the moments before as the silky fabric slid over her shoulders, cooling her.

Was this the reason she came to visit? To be close to him, to feel him kiss her again? Yes, she had to admit, it was a deciding factor. She needed the vacation as well, but she could have gone anywhere. Edmonton, to see her sister. Vancouver to go shopping. But she picked Blue River. She decided to stay and give it another chance. Maybe, just maybe, the two of them could sort this out as adults.

She heard him running the water to clean up the kitchen. She crawled under the covers and buried her head in the soft warmth of the homemade quilt.

Michael finished up just before eleven, after checking that everything was fine in the barn before walking wearily into the house. She had played havoc on his mind all evening and it was becoming quite clear that the attraction he had to her was more than purely physical. If it was only physical, he knew he would be in her bed right now, but something was stopping him and it wasn't her protests.

He pulled off his boots on the front porch steps before quietly opening the screen door. His sock feet made it easy to be quiet as he made his way up the narrow staircase to his room. He stopped for a moment at the top of the stairs, aware that Vanessa's door was slightly ajar. Taking a deep breath, he stepped toward it, still undecided as to whether or not he should touch it. His strong hand held the brass doorknob as he pushed the door gently inward. The curtains across the room blew softly. His gaze crossed to the semi-covered figure that lay on the bed in the middle of the room. He swallowed hard, aware of the feelings of arousal overcoming him as his eyes traced the delicate curve of her exposed shoulder. Silently he closed the door, knowing that if he didn't he would regret his actions in the morning.

Four

Vanessa awoke to the smell of cooked bacon wafting up the narrow staircase, permeating through the wooden door of the guest room. She was slightly disoriented for a few seconds before she fully awoke. Feeling the stiffness in her elbow, Vanessa suddenly recalled why it was bruised. The fresh country air flowed through the half-opened window, blowing the lace curtains gently inward.

A gentle tapping on her door made her fully realize where she was. "Vanessa, breakfast is ready. Get up, you're burning daylight, lady." The commanding voice was that of Michael, she realized, her heart suddenly lurching with the prospect of having to face him after their tussle last night.

"Be right down," she called back, searching the gigantic

bed for her robe. She only had a few minutes to make herself presentable or he might get the idea she didn't want to face him.

Vanessa listened, ears perked to hear his heavy footsteps head down the stairs, before she silently opened the bedroom door to head into the bathroom at the end of the hall. After a quick wash up she hastily brushed the braid that had remained almost intact last night. Her golden tresses fell softly in waves on her shoulders. Just a touch of blusher and mascara was all she needed to enhance her natural morning glow.

Back in her room she slipped into a clean pair of khaki pants and red tee-shirt. As she dressed, Vanessa considered what to say to Michael after last night. She thought he had understood she was here for a vacation, not looking for an affair. She was going to have to set him straight at the first opportunity. She gave herself the once over in the oval antique mirror that stood in the corner of the quaint room. It would have to do, she thought, as she glanced at her watch. Five minutes had passed and he would be waiting. She quickly pulled on cotton socks before walking down for breakfast.

She found him standing over the sink, pouring coffee into two mugs. Vanessa stopped to admire the tapered waist that fit smoothly into faded jeans. The blue checked shirt he wore yesterday was replaced by a red one. She smiled as she thought of the first time she laid eyes on this attractive man. She never would have guessed he could look so stunning in cowboy gear, but then again, he looked terrific in his suit and tie as well.

"Hi," she ventured softly, all thoughts of wanting just a vacation vanishing in an instant. Her awakening libido seemed to be one step ahead of her rational mind as she concluded that she would take things as they came, not worrying about the outcome. She was a grown woman, after all, she heard the little voice inside her head preaching.

"Good morning. Sleep well?" Michael quirked an eyebrow in her direction as he carried the coffees to the table already set with bacon and eggs, toast, jam and juice. She looked even sexier in the morning, her soft wavy hair floating around her face, making her look like the angel he was beginning to think she was. Damn, if he couldn't keep his growing desire in check whenever she entered a room!

"Yes, thanks." Vanessa took her seat at the table and watched as he eased himself into his own spot directly across from her.

Their eyes met over raised mugs of steaming coffee. In a split second both were apologizing for the night before.

"I'm sorry I chased you last night. I don't know what got into me," he started.

"I'm sorry. I guess I was a little shocked to have a full-grown man jump me at the top of the stairs." Vanessa laughed, a nervous sound that tickled the back of her throat. She rubbed her elbow unconsciously where it was tender from the bruise inflicted in the chase.

Michael smiled, admiring the way she handled herself this morning. He was afraid she might have had her bags packed and ready to leave before he had a chance to stop her. He had plans for her first day on the ranch.

"Would you like to see the ranch today, Vanessa? I've got some horses if you'd like to ride." He took another sip as he watched her pick at her breakfast, hoping she would say yes.

"Sure you want me to hang around?" she asked, hesitantly, pushing her eggs around on the full plate.

"Of course. It's your holiday and I want you to enjoy it. Right after breakfast I'll saddle up so we can spend most of the day out there. I've got a lunch already packed." Michael turned slightly pink under his tanned good looks, realizing she knew now that he had already planned that she would stay.

Vanessa laughed softly. "You sure think you've got me figured out, don't you?" She stared into his steel gray eyes, not allowing him to stare her down. She was going to show him she wasn't afraid of him, or his advances, but she let him know it would be on her terms. "Let me tell you something. I've been on my own for the last four years, and no man has even come close to having an effect on me like you do. You intrigue me," she admitted, "but I need time and space. If you are willing to give it to me, I think we could have a very enjoyable vacation."

He propped his elbows onto the small wooden table, resting his finely chiseled chin on his interlocked fingers. A slow smile crossed his face, his lips not parting until he spoke.

"You're fascinating to me, you know that?" he asked, studying the contours of her face.

She blushed, feeling flustered with his outright response. She never considered herself a fascinating woman.

"We actually have more in common than we think," Michael continued, determined to win her over. After the performance last night, he wasn't sure she would give him another chance so he jumped at the opportunity now.

"Really, like what?" she challenged. She took a bite of the delicious eggs he had prepared.

"Well, for starters, we both run our own companies. That must give us some common ground. And we both are single at the moment." His eyes held hers for a second, making her quiver inside with his deeply sensual gaze.

"Why aren't you attached?" Vanessa asked, reluctant to probe into his life so personally, but wanting to know more about him. She watched him with deep concentration. She imagined him with women in every city he traveled, and was suddenly overcome with unwarranted envy.

"I was once. It didn't work out." His tone was flat, undecipherable. She watched him in silence, waiting for an explanation. Michael knew about Mark, and he owed her this much. He continued. "She didn't like the country life, and I was too stubborn to change."

"Oh, and are you more susceptible to change, now that you're older? Would you be able to adapt to city life now?" she asked, staring directly into those cool gray eyes of his. How could she think of such things when really they were just friends, getting to know each other? Why did she suddenly find herself thinking 'commitment' with this handsome man?

"I'm not that much older now. Maybe wiser. But I wouldn't give this up." Michael waved his broad palm in the air, emphasizing his territory. "I'm thirty-five, and set in my ways."

"Yes, I guess I am, too. I love what I do and I don't think it would be easy to give up the business. It would certainly take the right man to make me leave it behind." Her playful smile was infectious. He watched her, mesmerized, as her smile lifted the corners of her pale rose lips. She had appeared in his life less than a week ago, and yet he knew he wanted her for the rest of time. He turned his attention to gathering the finished plates in front of them.

Together they cleared the dishes, placing them in the double sink. Vanessa settled in washing the plates while Michael grabbed a clean cloth from the tiny closet by the door. They chatted amicably, neither one mentioning the night before. Michael was given full warning at breakfast about how fast he could pursue her, and on what terms. He understood her request for time and space, but he didn't know how long he could hold out, waiting for her to come to him.

He looked down at her golden hair glittering in the morning sun. He felt his male desire rise in his tight jeans. Trying to rid himself of the uncontrollable urge to take her in his arms, he raised his head to peer out the window to distract himself. It had been a long time since he shared his kitchen with a woman, he thought, turning back to face her.

"I'll go round up the horses. When you're ready come down to the barn, and I'll show you how to saddle a horse. Do you have a hat? It looks like it may be a scorcher today."

"Yes, I brought one, and I can saddle my own horse, remember? I told you I grew up around horses."

"Right. I'll pack the lunch with me," he said, poking his head into the refrigerator. The brown paper bag containing the cheese, crackers, wine and tablecloth was still intact, rolled down to conceal its contents from her.

She watched him as he headed out the door, bag under one arm, cowboy hat in the other hand. He propped it over his eyes as he headed toward the barn. Major leaped up to sniff the contents of the bag before dashing ahead toward the barn. She should have asked him to keep the dog away from her, fearing another surprise attack. She laughed to herself, noticing that the dog and his master had similar traits when it came to women they wanted to get to know. She watched a moment longer, feeling the excitement of being able to ride again. She felt it was going to be a good vacation, as she went back upstairs to retrieve her hat and boots.

The sun was unseasonably warm for May as she walked across the stretch of dirt that separated the barn from the house. She assumed the huge mutt was with its owner in the barn, so she figured she was safe walking alone. Vanessa glanced up at the black clouds that were starting to form in the west, but paid little attention to them. Nothing was going to ruin a pleasant ride in the country for her.

"Michael," she called, poking her head into the stable doorway, eyes peeled for the dog. She was bracing herself for another attack and this time she vowed to be braver about it. After all, Major didn't really harm her last night, and her childish fear of dogs was just that, a childish fear.

"Over here," he replied, but not before she was pushed down hard on her rear by the overly-friendly mutt. Michael came racing out of the stable, bridle still in his hand, stopping suddenly in front of her.

He loomed over her pinned body for a split second before commanding the dog to heel. Reluctantly Major obeyed, his huge brown eyes full of apology. Michael offered her a hand which she refused, getting up on her own steam as she wiped her seat with a brisk movement.

"That darn dog," she sputtered. "You trained him well. Is there any way I can stop him before he ruins all the clothes I brought with me?" She was too surprised to be upset, especially when she knew Michael was right there to control the beast.

"Maybe I shouldn't tell you," he teased, but quickly changed his mind about his thoughts on her having no clothes left to wear. The sharp look she cast him as she stood looking at him angrily made him hastily explain how to handle the dog.

"Good, now let me try," she said, turning to face the black

and brown shepherd. Major sat obediently a few feet away. She copied the commands Michael gave and the dog responded properly.

"See, nothing to it." Michael told Major to stay and look after the place. Major gave a quick wag of his tail before heading to the front porch where he assumed his sleeping guard dog pose in the warm morning sun.

Michael led her to the open stable where a huge chestnut mare waited patiently in her stall. Vanessa stopped just outside the gate to admire the mare, who seemed to be sizing her up at the same time.

"She's beautiful. Where did you ever get her?"

"I bought her when I owned a stable in Langley."

Vanessa detected the melancholy tone to his voice, unsure if she should question him further, but her curiosity got the best of her. He had never mentioned the stable before, and the fact that he had owned one intrigued her. It had been a childhood dream of hers and here she was standing next to a man who had given it up.

"What made you decide to sell the stable and keep the ranch?" She watched him as he deftly handled the gentle mare. He held his hand for the soft nose to sniff.

"I don't remember now," he said, images of a failed marriage turning his heart cold. "I guess I'm really the country type." He smiled his gorgeous smile, making Vanessa tingle inside.

She wouldn't accept his seemingly off-the-cuff reply. She felt as if he was avoiding the subject, and she was curious as to why. As she shifted her weight onto one foot, she leaned against the stable door. "I would think owning a stable would be for the country type. Tell me what happened."

Michael stopped working with the saddle, giving her a cold glance. Noting the sudden widening of her eyes, he realized too late that it was just an innocent question. She really deserved an honest answer, no matter what he wanted to keep buried inside himself.

"If you have to know, my ex-wife and I owned the stable. I bought it before we married, as an investment, and to help pay my way through university. I loved the life surrounding the stable, but I guess I loved it more than her. She got lonely, and found someone who paid her a little more attention." The hurt still reflected in his steel gray eyes.

"So you divorced, and split the profits," she said softly. Vanessa's heart went out to him, wanting to heal the hurt that showed in his face. She accepted his nod as the end of the conversation. She continued studying him as he finished tightening the bridle. It had been years since she rode a horse. Before Mark died, she used to spend her days at the stables riding her own horse while he was away on business. The pungent smell of the barn brought back memories of the days when she was young and carefree, growing up on a farm in Nova Scotia.

Vanessa stepped up to the big rust-coloured mare and stroked the quivering neck gently while whispering in the attentive mare's ear. "What's her name? Rusty?" She made a light-hearted laugh as she peered over the horse's back to look directly at him.

"As a matter of fact, yes." His somber face broke into a wide grin, his eyes dancing in amusement. The tenseness of a few moments ago left him as he smiled at her.

Michael threw the saddle on Rusty's back, and before he had a chance to walk around her to cinch it on, he found Vanessa already busy with the buckle. Michael watched in amazement, wondering how a woman who could have such a fear of dogs be so unafraid of a horse.

As if knowing what he was about to ask, Vanessa filled him in. "I used to ride all the time when I was young. We always had two or three horses around. My parents still own the farm in Nova Scotia."

"Why the fear of dogs, then, when you're not afraid of horses?"

Vanessa grimaced. "I really don't know. My mother says I was jumped by a large dog when I was really young, just a toddler, but I don't remember. I guess it's something I'll never get over."

Michael nodded. "Ready?" he asked, holding the reins for her. She took a step forward to grab them, their hands touching briefly, creating the spark she was trying hard to avoid but finding impossible with him. She followed Michael as he led his dazzling black stallion out of the barn. If Rusty towered over her, Danny Boy, Michael's horse, loomed even larger.

Vanessa's heart thudded inside her, making her hands tremble in anticipation. She mounted the mare with remembered ease.

Michael gave an approving glance as she leaned forward to whisper in Rusty's ear, gently nudging her to follow Danny Boy, which the mare seemed to intend to do anyway.

The open road leading back to the highway had many trails breaking off into the sparsely treed area surrounding the Ryan ranch. Michael prodded his mount to a canter when he reached the open trail that led to the oasis of poplars on the hill in the distance.

The breeze created by the faster pace blew the wild curling wind around Vanessa's glowing cheeks. She should have tied her hair back or at least propped it up under her hat, but Michael was already far ahead. Vanessa nudged Rusty's ribs, urging her to close the gap between them. Rusty obliged willingly, catching Danny Boy much quicker than Vanessa expected. She clung to the racing thoroughbred with both knees pressed firmly against the mare. She was breathless when they caught up, reining in to fall in stride with Michael.

"She was born to run, wasn't she?" He grinned at her, watching the flushed face as it peeked through the mass of blonde hair that settled onto her shoulders as they slowed.

"She's terrific," Vanessa said, between gasps of air. "It's just that it's been so long…" She looked around, now able to hear the babbling of the brook he had led her to, after the glorious ride through the forest.

Michael studied her as she gazed around. Back erect, shoulders straight, she sat tall in the saddle. His gray eyes followed her gaze to the curve in the stream just ahead of them. The grassy field spread out from the banks, covered mostly in wild daisies that flourished in clumps sporadically in all directions. The openness of the field was surprising, given the mountainous terrain that surrounded them.

Michael knew she would like the serenity of this place. It was his favorite spot on the ranch when he needed someplace to be alone and think or dream. He remembered watching the field of daisies blow back and forth in a rhythm not unlike the slow medley of a love song.

Maybe Vanessa would be more receptive to his advances in the outdoors, closer to nature. At least, that was his hope. He planned the quiet picnic with just that in mind, but as he looked at her now, he knew he would have to go slow if he was going to get anywhere.

"Coming?" he asked, as he gracefully dismounted, leaving the reins to fall freely to the ground. Danny Boy gratefully acknowledged his chance to graze the tender greens of the field.

Trying to take her mind off the tension she felt just watching Michael's lean, muscular body dismount from the huge animal, Vanessa's thoughts wandered to business at home. It didn't work for more than a minute. Her eyes followed the broad-shouldered man as he walked up to the bend in the stream. She remained perched on her mount, not daring to move, knowing the ride would have made her legs wobbly for the next little while, or was it Michael who was making her feel weak?

He turned suddenly, aware that she was not right behind him. He waved a muscled arm for her to follow him. She was about to dismount when she glimpsed the tanned shoulders and back bare to the waist revealed when he removed the checkered shirt that had outlined his trim body so nicely. Her throat caught, dry from the ride, and the scene that unfolded before her. He was down to his shorts before she realized what he intended to do.

He caught her awed expression as she perched half on, half off her mount. He smiled a wry smile before diving into the cooling stream.

The sun beat down through the protective felt of her hat. Vanessa dismounted quickly, allowing Rusty the freedom to move closer to her mate. It was becoming unbearably hot.

He didn't tell her to pack a swimsuit, she thought, annoyed with him for tantalizing her. So much for taking his time and not rushing her. His striptease was not doing much for her resolve to take things slowly, to give the relationship time. The lace bra and panties she was wearing were not enough to pass as suitable attire to swim in, even though he seemed to have no problem jumping in with just his shorts on. Annoyance turned to frustration as she tried to concentrate on something other than the images unfolding before her. His lean, tanned body stretched into a perfect diving pose burned into her brain. She couldn't stop the thoughts of seeing him without his shorts, wondering if he actually had a tan on his whole body. She somehow suspected he did.

The thought of walking over to the pool and stripping to her undies in front of a man she had known for less than a week sent shivers of temptation coursing through her body. He would deserve to watch her as she removed her clothing by the side of the river, knowing that he only did it himself to tease her.

It had been a long, hot ride. Hearing the gentle lapping of his arms on the water as he swam in the wide pool only served to make her feel hotter. Turning her back to him, Vanessa stalked over to the edge of the stream where both horses were taking long drafts of the clear water. She rolled up her sleeves and bent down on her knees to splash the water on her burning face and arms. She used a flat rock as a seat and began to pull her boots and socks off, placing them neatly on the shore before rolling up her cuffs and dipping her hot, neatly shaped feet in to the welcoming water. She avoided looking upstream where she heard Michael swimming.

Finally Michael waded from the water and pulled his jeans on, leaving the belt undone as he reached for other clothes he left strewn over the grass. He had forgotten to pack a towel, and the wet outline of his shorts seeped through his jeans in a matter of minutes, but he somehow didn't think Vanessa would appreciate it if he walked back in his shorts. He chastised himself for not thinking ahead of time, telling her to bring a swimsuit, packing a towel. It felt good to cool off after the ride, and to quench the thirst that was building inside him for the woman who had walked into his life less than a week ago. He still couldn't believe she was here with him.

He watched her from the far side of his horse as he gathered the brown bag containing the ingredients of a romantic picnic he had packed earlier. Her back was to him, her hair whisked back behind the delicate ears, her feet still lolling in the water making a soft swishing sound. He walked twenty feet back from the stream, finding a shady spot under a clump of poplar trees. He spread the red and white checkered cloth on the soft grass, smoothing it out before placing the feast in the middle. The wine was still cool as he pulled the two glasses off the neck, laying them beside the bottle.

He stood up to pull his shirt back on, his body dried by the sun and the breeze now. Vanessa turned in time to see the long arms pushed into the sleeves, seams stretching to their limits as he started to button the front. He didn't notice her watching him until he unzipped his pants to tuck the shirt in.

Vanessa quickly turned her head, the flush sure to show twenty feet away, she thought, as she tried to hide her face in the mass of hair that blew in the breeze.

"You must have seen a man dress before," he yelled across to her, making her cringe even deeper into the ball she was trying to become. Her insides ached with the longing to see more of the man who walked silently toward her in his bare feet.

He was behind her now, so close he could touch her shining hair, but he didn't. Instead, he rolled up his cuffs and nestled himself on the rock beside her.

She reached into the shallow pool, picking a colourful rock out of the still water as she tried to compose herself. The sight of him half-naked and his offhanded remark brought back old memories of Mark she thought she had buried years ago. The idea of starting a new relationship with a man she knew she wanted scared her. She had already lost Mark, and there was no turning back the pages of time. Her life had to continue, but what if something happened to Michael? She didn't know if she could handle it. Once was enough. Quickly she wiped at her eyes as Michael joined her.

Shifting his weight onto the flat rock she occupied, he reached over to inspect the rock she turned in her hand. At the same time she twisted to pull away, knocking him flat in the water, soaking his jeans and most of his shirt in the process.

She laughed at the shocked look on his face, then quickly offered her hand before thinking of the consequences. He might not have pulled her in if she hadn't laughed, but since she did, he figured she deserved it. She landed beside him on the sandy shoal, the shock of the cold water making her gasp for breath.

"Why, you—" she started, as he reached to pin her flailing arms before she could inflict more pain on him. His lower body ached from the sudden stop on the round, flat rocks and it hurt to move too quickly.

He gazed into the flashing green eyes, unable to read what she was feeling, trying to find the answer to the sudden tears. His lips moved to hers, making her fall silent, as he gently kissed her, moving to her jawline and down her delicate throat. Vanessa moaned as she closed her eyes, feeling the heat rise as she sat submerged in the cold water.

Her arms went around his neck as he lifted her out of the stream. For her height, she was not as heavy as he would have expected, even though she was soaking wet. She buried her face in the damp collar of his shirt, deeply breathing the intoxicating smell she remembered from their night in the rain.

She returned his gentle kisses, opening her mouth to his prodding tongue. He groaned as she moved her hands down his muscled back to his waist. He pressed himself tighter against the hard nipples of her breasts, making him feel the tightness in his damp jeans.

Vanessa laid back on the tablecloth where he had deposited

her. He gently brushed the hair out of her eyes, which now were dark pools of emeralds. Vanessa allowed the slow, gentle stroking of his fingers to linger on her face and down her neck. Her breathing quickened as he pulled himself closer, almost on top of her as he lowered his face to hers. His breath was hot as he nibbled at her earlobe, making her close her eyes to give herself up to the wonderful feelings that flooded through her. Reading her submissiveness as a go-ahead to continue his exploration of the sensuous creature that lay beneath him, Michael unzipped the pants she wore, sliding his hot, probing fingers into the fuzzy mat that covered her most hidden parts. She couldn't deny the feelings she had tried to suppress the past few days, but the danger of jumping into an affair without due consideration of the consequences made her stiffen to his gentle touch.

"What's wrong?" he asked, feeling her tighten as he pressed himself closer to her.

"I...I'm not ready for this," she gasped, hoping she wasn't scaring him off. He was too attractive for her own good, she thought, as she watched him straighten up and shove away from her to the other side of the tablecloth.

"Honey, I can't hold out forever." He stared at her intently, his steel gray eyes piercing her heart.

"Neither can I," she whispered, surprising herself with her forthright response. They sat in awkward silence for a moment before Michael leaned over and kissed her forehead. Taking the wine bottle in his powerful hands, Michael diverted his attention to opening it.

Vanessa busied herself with the cheese and crackers, getting a few ready to eat. She was famished, she realized, from the fresh, sexually charged air surrounding them. She held out the two glasses as the plastic cork popped into the leaves above them.

"To us," Michael toasted, clinking his glass to hers. He leaned back to settle himself on one elbow, watching Vanessa across from him. His eyes roamed the length of her soaked jeans, slowly following the outline of her wet shirt, her nipples taut against the lacy outline of her bra, which didn't do a thing to relieve the pressure of his erection.

Vanessa shivered, not sure if it was from the chill of the water or his approving look. The warmth of the sun dipped behind a fluffy gray cloud momentarily darkening the field.

He moved closer to her, placing the open bottle against the smooth stone beside the tablecloth. Vanessa snuggled in closer, keeping the snacks balanced on her lap as he covered her shoulder protectively against the cooling breeze.

She offered him one of the prepared snacks, holding the morsel delicately between her fingers. His lips were electric to her touch as he consumed the cracker. He grabbed her wrist with his free hand. He swallowed quickly, placed her fingers in his mouth and gently licked her fingertips, one at a time. He turned her hand over to inspect the palm, caressing the smooth lines with his warm tongue, running the length of her exposed arm.

Vanessa shivered again, fascinated with the erotic effect of his touch. Reaching behind her, she placed her glass beside the one he had previously deposited, hardly noticing if they stayed put.

She deftly moved the edibles to the rock beside her, allowing the two of them to curl up together on the now rumpled tablecloth. The warmth from Michael's body penetrated the length of her front, from chest to toes. She snuggled closer as he reached for the edge of the cloth to wrap over her shivering shoulders. The clouds that threatened earlier gobbled what little warmth was left from the sun.

"Maybe we better continue this at home," Michael said, placing his firm hand on her chin. Her green eyes sparkled like the glittering brook beside them, trying to hide the chill of the afternoon breeze.

"I...I think you're right," she said, through chattering teeth. They scrambled for the horses left standing under a group of poplars. The rain started to drizzle as Michael tied the picnic, hobo-stick-style to the saddle horn. It was going to have to be a fast hour's ride back if they were going to make it back before the thunderclouds erupted, he thought, studying the rolling blackness that crept in quickly from the west.

Vanessa was struggling to get her boots on as she stood beside Rusty, one hand pressed against the warm, muscular leg of her mount. The next second, she found herself flung to the ground as Rusty bolted at the cracking sound of thunder that carried across the darkened sky. Vanessa scrambled up almost as quickly as she had fallen, glancing around as if trying to figure out what happened.

Michael reached over from his vantage point on Danny Boy's back and touched Vanessa's shoulder. "Come on. We'll both ride Danny Boy," he urged as he watched Rusty race ahead to the shelter of the barn. The rain started to pelt down even as he spoke. He reached down to grasp her outstretched hand as she struggled to get her foot in the stirrup he vacated for her. As she swung her leg over, she felt the heat from his back penetrate against her breast as she settled behind him. The only part that managed to stay dry on Vanessa was the hair under her hat. She clung to Michael, feeling the thud of his heartbeat as he rode his stead at a steady, galloping pace.

Vanessa steadied herself as she held tightly to his ribs. The up and down motion of the ride caused her already soaked breasts to chafe against his taut, wet back, hardening her nipples until she almost cried out in raptured pleasure. She envisioned him her knight in shining armor, rescuing her and sweeping her away to his castle. He certainly was shining, rain streaming down the back of his hat splashed onto his soaked shirt, outlining the tight muscles that worked the horse so well. The landscape was a fuzzy blur as Vanessa focused her attention on the back of his neck.

The barn loomed up quicker than she expected even though it had been almost an hour's ride. Although the rider behind usually dismounts first, Michael quickly swung a long leg over Danny Boy's quivering neck so he could help her get down from the tall animal. He raised his arms to catch her as she swung her leg over the horse's neck, sliding into his strong arms easily. The wetness of his shirt met her scantily clad upper body with a soft squish as he pulled her close to him.

She felt the fire rise inside her as his hands roamed the length of her back, gently pulling her closer. She could smell the scent of horses and rain, a tantalizing mixture that made her senses come alive in the chill of the afternoon shower. He gently kissed her waiting mouth before speaking.

"You better get in and run a hot bath. You're turning blue. I'll be in as soon as I take care of the horses."

"I can help. I used to do this all the time," she said, ignoring his steel gray eyes as they bored into the back of her head. She knew if she looked at him there would be no arguing about his preference. Rusty was already waiting in her stall.

"Okay." He quickly wiped Danny Boy down, giving her one of the towels to do the same to her mount. He finished a few seconds before her, surprised at the skill she showed in taking care of such a majestic animal. Vanessa caught his admiring glance, and returned it with a bright smile. Michael finished putting the tack away, closing the gate to each of the stalls before approaching her.

"So, we have one more thing in common," she said, laughing and shivering at the same time. Her hair hung in her eyes as she tried unsuccessfully to push it away.

"Allow me," he said, brushing his wet hand against her forehead before he gently grazed her lips with his own wet ones. The sharp bristle that was growing back from his early shave this morning grazed her soft skin. His warm breath caressed her face as he held her chin in his tight grasp. Vanessa returned his embrace, running her hands through his tangled mass of hair, pulling it as her fingers caught in the mess.

"Sorry," she murmured between breaths. Her breathing was rapid now, the coldness of her wet body seeming to disappear magically. Her shivers were now caused by internal reactions to his aggressiveness.

Pleasure gave way to common sense as Michael picked her up and carried her across the yard to the warmth of the waiting house. He desperately wanted to make love to her in the hay of the empty stable, but now wasn't the time, he told himself.

Five

The pounding of the rain was barely audible over the sound of water running into the immensely deep bathtub. Vanessa had never bathed in a tub so old or so large. The claw feet were made of highly polished brass. The enamel outside and in was smooth for the most part. A few chips near the faucets made its authenticity ring true.

Vanessa slipped silently into its welcoming warmth, bubbles covering her to her chin. She wondered about the person who installed the tub originally, picturing someone as tall or taller than Michael. Surely someone of less stature would never have any desire to drown in such luxury. Her feet barely reached the end as she slid herself deeper into the tub.

Closing her eyes, Vanessa allowed the warmth to penetrate

her cold fingers and legs. The blue colour Michael had noticed was certainly there. She held up her delicate hands for closer inspection. She smoothed the silky water over her face and neck. It felt good to be warm again. She was almost lulled to sleep as the pounding rain subsided to a gentle pattering against the high window.

Michael. Just the thought of him made her insides stir as if they were awakening on demand. A twinge of guilt flashed through her as she remembered the last few years with Mark. The spark had nearly died before he did, and she couldn't remember ever feeling the same chemistry she felt now between Michael and herself. With Michael, the fire was there, in his smoldering gray eyes, in his strong embrace. Mark had always seemed distracted when they made love and she admitted it hurt to think she may not have known true love with Mark when she thought she had.

Realization suddenly dawned as she thought about the differences between the two men. She had once loved Mark, attracted to him by his quick wit and intelligence. But over the years he became more interested in his business than in her. He never took her on his many business trips, telling her she would be bored, or the stay was too long to take her.

Michael, on the other hand, wanted her with him. After all, he had invited her to visit his ranch. The attraction she had for him was mirrored in his reaction to her. And a powerful one it was, too. She knew this by his many overtures toward her.

But still she held back from him. It wasn't that she didn't want him. She craved him, and she knew it. Just thinking about how he would feel inside her, his hot tongue probing the depths of her mouth and on her teeth, his fingers reaching into her more intimate, but responsive area made her quiver. She closed her eyes as she ran her hands over her breasts and across her belly, longing for them to be his hands.

The muffled sounds of Michael moving about in the kitchen brought Vanessa out of the pleasant dream. She wasn't sure it was a dream, it seemed so real. The soft scent of the bouquet of flowers Michael had placed in the room this morning wafted in the steamy room. She strained to hear his footsteps crossing the expansive kitchen floor and when the stairs creaked under his weight, she slipped into the tepid depths of the water, knowing it was Michael coming to tell her to relinquish the tub to him.

She wasn't prepared for the intrusion into her privacy when Michael barged in, his huge frame looming over her as he stepped to the sink.

"Oh," she gasped, splashing some of the now tepid water over the side of the old tub. She covered her bare chest with crossed arms, feeling the flush rise from her exposed rib area to the top of her head.

"Oh," he echoed. "Sorry, I thought you'd be finished by now." His soft chuckle resonated in the small room.

Vanessa relaxed, sinking under the cover of disappearing bubbles. "That's okay. You just surprised me, that's all."

"Mind if I join you?" he asked, his eyes warming with obvious intent.

"It's getting cool," she started, reaching for the faucet to add more hot water. He reached her arm in time to stop her. A hot jolt charged through her entire body, making her jump visibly. Her exposed breasts rose in rhythm to the rapid breathing she tried to control as Michael softly ran his finger up the length of her arm and across her back. The touch relaxed her as if he had placed a magic spell over her. Vanessa wanted nothing more than to pull him into the bath with her and have him do what he liked with her unfulfilled body.

Vanessa knew Michael was the one she wanted, but she still hesitated to tell him. What if he turned out to be like Mark, she wondered, consumed more with his business than with being with her. She was right to take her time, she warned herself. The one little voice fought the other as she struggled to control the situation.

As if sensing her apprehension, Michael backed off. She had told him she needed time, and he wasn't going to rush her, no matter how urgent he felt the need, which seemed to be every time he saw her.

"I'll let you finish here," he said. He placed a big, fluffy towel on the toilet lid, within her reach. Michael crossed the hall to his room. He undressed quickly, allowing the soaked clothes to fall to the floor in a heap. He would do laundry before supper, but right now he had to get warm. A romp in the tub with Vanessa was the best way to get the circulation back into his cold limbs, but he didn't want to force the issue. He still felt the burning on his lips from their caresses in the field, and later in the barn.

Michael was dressed in a clean pair of jeans, warm socks, and cream fisherman knit sweater. Nothing looked bad on him, Vanessa thought, walking into the kitchen intending to help with supper.

"Just about done here," he said, his back to her as he placed something into the oven. "Hope you like frozen lasagna. Well, cooked frozen lasagna." He turned to face her, casserole in hands, waiting for her reply. Instead, he caught the look of horror on her face a split second before the overgrown puppy jumped on her for the third time in two days.

"Major," he yelled, dropping the dish on the floor at the same time. He was torn between rescuing their supper, and rescuing her, but only for an instant. He hauled the big brute off her as she sputtered and wiped her face with the clean sleeves of her cotton blouse.

"Damn, that dog," he cursed, pushing the reluctant furry mass out the porch door. "Are you all right?" He offered his hand, but she batted it away.

"Michael Ryan, if you can't do something with that dog," she started. "Ahh, just look at me. This was the last clean casual outfit I packed," she added, swiping madly at the dirty paw prints left on her chest.

"Hold on," he said. "I'll get you something."

He appeared a moment later with a pair of jeans, well-worn, and a dark green turtleneck sweater for her to put on. "They belong to Les' granddaughter."

Her eyes widened, wondering why he would have Les' granddaughter's clothes but was afraid to ask.

As if to cover himself, he added hastily, "They were left behind the last time Becky was here. Les thought I might drop them off the next time I was in Vancouver. I should have mailed them. He always hoped we would hit it off, but she's not my type."

She smiled, satisfied with the explanation, but embarrassed that he felt he had to explain. "I'll go change." She clutched the clean clothes to her breast, turning to head up the narrow staircase to the privacy of her room.

Michael followed her gently swaying hips with his eyes, feeling the swelling in his pants take a life of its own. "Two months ago I thought you were dead," he whispered, rearranging himself in his groin area before returning to the supper that he managed to ruin.

Michael cleaned up the last of the lasagna and tossed it into the garbage under the sink. Now he would have to start from scratch and make something else if he was going to feed her properly or they would have to dine out, he realized.

The drive to the nearest restaurant was over two hours. When faced with the choice, Vanessa opted to try and help prepare something from what was left in the fridge. She was a whiz at whipping up a creamy macaroni dish, full of goodies he never imagined using. She took over his kitchen with ease, sending him down the hall to the main bathroom for a quick, hot shower. He didn't argue. She knew how to handle herself in the kitchen, and everything was under control.

Michael relaxed in the steamy warmth of the shower. His thighs ached from the hard ride in the rain. The cold had penetrated to the bone, but he hadn't realized it until now.

He closed his eyes, blocking out any thoughts of Vanessa. But he could still feel her presence as he reached down to turn the setting to warm.

Vanessa knocked hard on the wooden door. "Five minutes to supper." Then she headed upstairs to grab her pocketbook before he got out.

"Thanks, be right out," he said as he quickly stepped out of the shower and dried himself off roughly. Then he sauntered down the hall and up the stairs to his room wearing nothing but his towel. His hair was still damp, with the straight strands tousled all over.

Vanessa emerged from her room and gasped at seeing his almost naked body for the second time today, but this time it was up close. He stopped short, not expecting her to be standing in the hallway.

"I…I just had to get my book," she explained hastily. His deeply sensual laugh filled the narrow hallway. She flushed, realizing she was staring at his perfect, masculine body, glistening with dampness, as he stood outlined in his doorway. Beyond him she noticed the pine chest of drawers, the wooden floor adorned with a handsome homemade rug, the drawn curtains. Along the wall below the curtains stood a massive display of books next to the desk that held his computer.

"I see you have a computer," she said, trying to take her mind off his masculine, totally sexy body.

"Take a look," he said, beckoning her inside. It was too late to turn down the invitation to his room. She was always curious about computers, and followed him inside. He flipped the switch for the computer and sat down in front of it. All she could see of him now was the broad, naked shoulders and muscular legs on either side of the chair. She held her breath, walking slowly. The girlish feeling of being in a boy's room for the first time surfaced uncontrollably.

Plopping herself on the hard bed across from his desk, she suddenly realized what she was sitting on and jumped up unexpectedly. Michael jerked his head to see what she was doing. She flushed deeply.

"Would you like my chair?" he asked, rising to meet her almost eye to eye. He stood in front of her, not two feet away, the smell of his clean skin making her breathe deeper and faster.

"No, that's all right. I don't know much about…"

She didn't get a chance to finish her sentence as he covered her quickly moving lips with his own. His tongue searched for hers as her mouth opened willingly.

"Vanessa," he whispered, "I can't wait forever."

She ran her fingers down his muscular neck, working the taut muscles into relaxed ones. Her hands slid down the silky skin of his back as his muscles flexed with the movement of his own arms across her back.

"Then we better stop," she murmured, "before there's no turning back."

He pulled away from her, his lips still burning with unquenched desire. The molten steel glazed his eyes as he held her face in his hands.

"When you're ready," he replied tensely. Vanessa pressed her soft blonde tresses into his chest. The guilt of denying the pleasure they both sought in each other weighed heavily on Vanessa. She felt she was leading him on, but the struggle inside her to give him what he desired raged on. She wasn't prepared for an affair, if that was what it would be, and she had not faced the possibility of commitment she wasn't sure she, or he, was ready for. She wiped the tears that trickled down her cheeks, wishing she could figure out what she wanted, and soon. Her body was ready—ready, willing and able—but she sensed he could read the mental parts of her as well as the obvious physical desires.

"I wish I trusted myself more," she whispered. She pulled away from his chest, his arms still wrapped tightly around her slim waist. She continued as he held her patiently. "It's just that, well…" she said, finding the words difficult.

He lifted her face up with one hand under her chin. "You don't know if you can trust me with your heart, right?" She nodded, biting her lower lip as the words echoed her feelings. "You have to live your life, Vanessa. It's the only one you're given. Don't waste it on tainted memories."

Vanessa wondered how he was so perceptive when it came to such deep thoughts. "What makes you think my memories are tainted?" she asked defensively.

"Remember, I was married once. I lost her, too, in a way, although she is still alive. But I still feel guilty sometimes that things never worked out for us. Maybe if I tried a little harder, but that's not the way things were. I've learned to accept that. You have to, too."

"Mark took such good care of me. It wasn't fair that he died so young. He had everything going for him, for us."

"You can't blame yourself for his death. That's just a part of life. My grandmother always had the right answer to everything, but when she died, I thought nothing would ever be right again. I've learned that I was wrong. It took a few years, but I've learned to accept life for what it gives. You can, too, Vanessa, if you just let it." He kissed her gently on the blonde bangs that wisped across her forehead.

Vanessa sniffed. "I know what you're saying, but it is so hard sometimes."

"You can't always take the easy way out. You can't run forever."

"I know," she whispered.

"Come on. Let me get dressed and we'll tackle that scrumptious smelling dinner you put together." He released her from his grip.

"I'll get it out of the oven this time. I don't think I can wait any longer if supper hits the floor again," she teased. Her good humor was returning, as she walked quickly from his room. Michael gazed after her, the front of his towel tightened in response to his thoughts about how those swaying hips would feel under the bed sheets.

After dinner, they cleared the table together, then headed into the cozy living room. Vanessa's mood was improving by the minute. She was not sure if it was the wine Michael opened for dinner, or the quiet comfort of knowing she was gaining a friend. They chatted about her business, how it was doing, where she was headed with it.

"Mark opened the business when the music box industry was barely known in Canada. He saw the opportunity in it, and I watched him nurture it as if it was a baby." She sighed, shifted her legs up underneath her on the cozy couch, then continued. "It was his baby, really, the only one he had any time for. It was lucky we didn't have any children," she added, "because he rarely was home. The company reaches the Saskatchewan border, but he had plans of going into Ontario in the next two years, had he not been killed."

"Are you going to expand it yourself?" he asked, refilling her glass as it rested on the pine table by the sofa.

"Yes, I'd like to." Vanessa caught the sudden darkness that clouded his eyes for a second before he glanced toward the fire. He rose to place another birch log on the fire. The flames leapt instantly, eating the dry bark hungrily.

Michael knew he wanted her, but she would have to be willing to live with him. He knew he couldn't give up the ranch life for the city. He decided to forget about it right now, try to enjoy the moments they could spend together, but the thought of losing her gnawed at the pit of his stomach.

"You look awfully pensive," she said, reaching for the hand he held outstretched to her. He gently pulled her onto the warm, vibrantly coloured oriental rug that covered most of the living room floor. Its richness contrasted with the muted shades of blue and gray, but somehow it tied the whole room together.

"It's nothing," he said, gently stroking her soft blonde hair with his hand. Vanessa smiled, and snuggled in closer to him on the rug. Her small, firm breasts crushed against his muscled chest as he pulled her tighter to him. He threw a heavy thigh over her own, gathering her into his growing arousal.

"Do you remember where we left off before the rain this afternoon?" he said, huskily.

"I think I was trying to wrap the tablecloth around us."

"It's too warm to wrap up in anything now," he said, his voice deeply suggestive.

She reached up to stop his hand from slowly driving her crazy with his gentle stroking. The fire sparkled in the gray eyes, making them almost golden in colour. She could feel the heat in the room, and not all of it was rising from the fireplace.

Time to make up your mind, girl, she told herself. It was going to be next to impossible to hold this virile man off much longer and she knew she wasn't going to be able to go back herself once they started. It was up to her, and it was time, she told herself. In fact, it was what everyone had been telling her. She was just too stubborn to admit it.

Getting up onto her knees, she shifted around to kneel behind him, placing her hands around his neck to tenderly rub his shoulders. She felt his muscles relax under her gentle massage. Leaning back slightly onto her calves, she pulled his head and shoulders into her lap.

He moaned softly as she rubbed his temples. Her soft touch was hardly noticeable as she lifted him off her lap and lowered him gently to the floor. "Now roll over," she whispered. Michael obeyed, stretching his arms before placing them under his chin, turning his head to look at her.

"Feels good?" she asked, swinging her right leg over the small of his back, her thighs pressing tightly against his ribs.

"Mmm," he murmured, as she worked the kinks out of his broad back.

"Take off your shirt now," she ordered. He responded promptly, tipping her onto the cozy rug, as he rolled over to a sitting position.

He laughed at the sight of her sprawled onto the floor, one leg trapped under his heavy thigh. "Sorry," he said, offering a hand to set her upright. "I guess I'm just not used to this."

"I wasn't finished yet," she quipped. "But if you are going to continue to pin me down every chance you get, I can guarantee you won't get another chance like this one. Now lie down," she commanded, placing her hands on her hips in a mocking pose.

"Whatever you say, ma'am," he said. His lips curled into a silly grin. She was making him feel warm inside, and he fought to control the urge to take her into his arms. She was the aggressor now, he thought, and he wasn't going to ruin it by forcing himself on her before she was ready.

The weight of her body rising and falling on his thighs in rhythm to her massaging fingers made his breathing become erratic until he could no longer stand her hot fingers running the length of his bare neck and sides.

Vanessa stopped for an instant to admire the smooth skin which rippled over well-toned muscles. Michael grabbed the moment to take control, rolling her off his back with one easy movement.

In the next second he loomed over her, straddling her, holding her firmly, pinning her with his thighs. He smoothed back the golden hair that fell in disarray, glowing warmly in the firelight.

Vanessa held her breath as she studied the tawny glow on the patch of dark hair that sprouted on his chest. Reaching up, she ran her hands over his shoulders and behind his neck, making him tighten his chest as he groaned deeply, waiting for her next move. She pulled him closer, tugging on his neck.

He bent down lower to gently kiss her, first on the forehead, warmed by the fire and heat brewing inside her. He followed the contour of her cheek, leaving a tingling trail with his mustache along her graceful neck.

Slowly one roughened hand worked its way along her ribcage, underneath the warm sweater. He found the gentle peaks of her breasts, rubbing his thumb across them back and forth, making her awakening nipples rise at his command.

Vanessa moaned, and pulled his mouth to hers. He pressed his full weight to her, kissing her more urgently now.

He stopped long enough to pull her on top of him while they continued their passionate caresses. She felt the warm hands pull the sweater over her shoulders. They broke for a second as he took the sweater off her completely, joining again hungrily, as he tossed the garment beside him.

Vanessa's heart pounded. She was very aware where they were heading, wanting him to occupy the aching emptiness that had been with her for too long. She realized they hadn't discussed the possibility of going that far, and she felt panic rise as she struggled to escape his grip. The thought of carrying protection had never occurred to her until this very moment.

"Michael, we can't," she gasped, between ragged breaths. "I'm not taking any precautions," she whispered, a slow heat rising to enhance the already visible glow in her pretty face.

"I already thought about that," he said. He gently lifted her off him. In one smooth movement he picked her up in his arms, her long legs dangling as she grabbed behind his neck, looping her arms around him, breathing in the heated scent of their passion.

Michael carried her with ease up the endless stairs, working the doorknob to his room with a quick twist. The door flew open, banging against the wall, as he strode to the oversized bed. He turned to sit down, still holding her in his arms. He wanted to ask if she was sure this was what she wanted but he was afraid all her old apprehensions would surface again and she would fight him, so he didn't. Instead he held her comfortably in his lap, tilting her chin to face his intense expression.

Taking a deep breath as if in answer to his unspoken words, her breasts rose in their lacy captivity. Struggling with the needs that were so evident now, she stared into the handsome, waiting face.

"I'm not the kind of person who just jumps into the bed with anyone."

"I can tell that," he said, huskily. The rough growth of beard scraped her jaw as he nuzzled her ear, as his hands deftly released the clasp on her bra. Her breath quickened as his big hands ran the length of her back, tenderly rubbing her hip, pulling her closer as he removed her bra.

"Michael, I need you," she panted with hot breath into his ear. As if in response to her acclamation, he stood her up on unsteady legs, expertly unzipping the pants she wore. The pants and panties slid off her slightly rounded hips, falling in a heap at her ankles. She raised her leg for him to pull off the sock in the same motion he used to remove the pant leg. He repeated the same procedure before sitting back on the bed, admiring the tawny glow of her skin in the evening light.

Vanessa shivered inwardly, watching him watch her. Never before had she experienced the pleasure of watching a man's face as he admired her feminine attributes. Not even Mark. In the next moment, she heard the quick zip and the heavy belt buckle as his jeans hit the floor in front of her.

Michael stood motionless in front of her. It was his turn to witness the pleasure in her face as she admired the healthy tone of his lean, muscular legs. She thought they would never stop until her hungry eyes reached his mid-section, confirming his obvious desire for her. Vanessa swallowed as her eyes flew to his face, waiting for him to make the next move.

He grabbed her by the wrists, pulling her back onto his bed. Reaching up, he cupped her breasts as she perched on top of him. Their firmness swelled in his gentle touch as he raised his lips to suckle one nipple, then the other.

She threw her head back, eyes closed, as she moaned in sheer delight when his one hand reached between her legs, searching for her hidden depths. Her own hand found the firmness of his erection, grasping him with her soft fingers, gently stroking him until he could wait no longer.

Vanessa rolled onto her back as he reached into the night table drawer to retrieve the package he had placed there a few days before. She heard the soft rip of the foil in the semi-darkness before his large hands gently glided over her inner thighs as he sought her warm, waiting femininity.

She gasped as he entered her, sending hot spasms of fire through her aching body. Her nails dug into his muscular shoulders as she arched herself to meet his increasing force. The soft flapping of the curtains in the breeze was barely audible over her passionate cries as she clung to the man she knew she wanted as they explored the depths of each other's desires.

She awoke in the silent darkness. Her chest ached, as if pinned under a scratchy log. In her semi-conscious state she tried to push the branch out of her way, struggling to push it off her body, trying to get free.

The branch twisted as she struggled, encircling her waist, capturing her. Her forehead felt cool as she broke into a sweat, pushing her torso off the spongy earth, nervously glancing around the unfamiliar darkness. She searched the sky with straining eyes, seeking the moon or stars. Nothing. Her breath came in short gasps as she lay shivering, her arms crossing her naked breasts.

A small scream escaped her parched lips. The branch she had dreamed was broken, suddenly came to life, running its leafy tendrils along her cool arm.

Michael stopped his attempt to comfort the woman who was crying softly as she lay curled in his arm, her head resting on his shoulder. Her sudden jolt to sit upright in the middle of the night put him off guard. This beautiful woman who had given herself so freely to him only hours ago, gentle and reassuring, was now more like a caged animal, desperate to be free.

He rubbed her shivering shoulder as she sat, her bare back straight and tight.

"It's okay. You're all right," he soothed, easing her back onto the pillow. In the darkness he found her lips, calming her with his warm kisses. "I love you," he murmured, but she had already drifted back into peaceful sleep, unable to respond to him.

Vanessa awoke late Monday morning, aware of the delicious scent of the previous night's lovemaking as she pulled the cozy comforter around her bare shoulders. She rolled onto her stomach to check the time on the clock on the nightstand beside her.

It was almost ten. The morning was half gone, and she had spent it asleep. She glanced around the room, aware suddenly that it was not the one she had slept in her first night at the ranch. A slow heat rose in her face as she contemplated how she was going to broach the subject of their affair to him. After all, that was what it must be. A torrid affair. The attraction was too great for any normal man and woman to withstand, so they merely gave in to their needs. It felt wonderful.

Her stiff, aching body cried out in satisfied pain. The muscles in her upper legs, tight from the night's tussle, and the horse ride earlier, screamed as she bent down to pick up the rumpled remnants of the clothes she wore last night. Gingerly she pulled on her underwear, socks, and pants. Before her sweater could be found, Michael announced his presence by presenting her with the woolly garment.

"You left this downstairs," he said, leaning against the door frame of his room. His eyes sparkled as he waited for her to respond.

"Thank you." She pulled the green bundle of warmth over her head. He watched her blonde head appear, much like a baby being born.

Not being able to control himself any longer, he clutched her in his arms, pressing the length of his body into her perfectly fitting curves. He kissed her hard on the mouth, breathing in the soft aroma of the warmth they shared last night. Had he actually said he loved her last night? Or did he just dream it? She certainly was everything he wanted in a woman, passionate and warm, a bit temperamental, but possessing a love of life. He shook the thoughts from his head, dreading the possibility that he was already in love with a woman who might eventually leave him. Better not to become too attached, he thought as he gently pulled himself away from her.

Vanessa's pulse raced as she felt the now familiar stirring, aware of how very much she wanted him. Her hair grazed the strong arm that held her head only a moment ago as she felt him push her away from the inviting warmth of his body. She moaned softly. A deep, muffled sound escaped her throat.

"Michael, we have to talk," she whispered, her heart pounding louder than she could ever remember, filling her ears with a roaring sensation.

"I know. But not now. I've got breakfast ready, and it's going to get cold if we stay here much longer." His eyes betrayed his preference for her over the warm breakfast.

She followed him out of the bedroom, feeling the heat rise in her again as she held the urge to touch him, make him touch her in the places he did last night. She ran her fingers through her hair, noticing how badly she needed to straighten herself up before starting the day with the most virile man she had known.

She couldn't bring herself to confront him about their affair and he seemed very quiet this morning except for the offer to take her for a drive into town to see the local sights. She agreed, feeling she would be safer in a Jeep than on a horse. Her legs would appreciate the chance to sit, and she hadn't had much of a chance to see the beauty of the Blue River country at all on her drive down.

She ate in silent resignation that, yes, it was an affair they were having. Never before had she slept with a man before a commitment was made. It would only serve to make her miserable if she spent any time dwelling on the fact.

Six

Theirs was the only vehicle on the road from the ranch to the turnoff onto the Highway 5 that ran north to Tete Jaune and south to Kamloops. Vanessa watched the ever-changing mountain scenery whiz by. She breathed in the sweet smell of the foliage through the open Jeep. Her hair started out tied back, now whipped around her eyes. She held it back with one hand for the last twenty minutes until she thought there was no blood left in her arm.

The sound of the engine blocked any chance for conversation. Michael was glad of it because he was still struggling with the way he wanted to approach her on the subject that had been on his mind since early this morning. Knowing she was sleeping soundly in his bed while he made breakfast was a comfortable feeling, something he could live with. But would she be willing to give up her work for him? It scared him just to think she might say no.

He stole a glance of her face as she watched the road. Her green eyes glittered in the rays of sun that mixed with the shadow of the trees as they sped along the narrow highway. Her lips were tight as if struggling with the wind in a battle to part them. Only he could win that battle, he thought, a slow smile crossing his own lips. The thought of tasting those very lips right now was making him hard.

He slowed the roaring vehicle as he drove through the townsite. Vanessa watched his strong arm gear down as he approached the turnoff to the little restaurant he had promised to take her to. It was a quaint loghouse-style building, with a sleeping dog on the front porch. Vanessa stiffened at the sight of the mangy old dog. This place seemed to be overrun with big dogs.

Michael noticed the apprehension on her face. He reached over to touch the tousled strands that fell in every direction except the right one.

"What's wrong?"

"Oh, nothing really. Just that dog," she said, pointing to the front steps of the restaurant.

"That's Ol' Yeller," he said. "Great guard dog. Deaf as a doorknob, and can't smell either. Come on." He hopped out his side with athletic ease, walked rapidly in front of the heated vehicle and promptly opened her door.

Vanessa climbed down with the helping hand he offered. She grabbed her woven bag from the back before falling in stride with his long steps. Walking beside him was a comfortable feeling, one she knew she would miss when she returned home. But she had business to take care of, she reminded herself. She was actually considering leaving this evening so that she could catch up on the week's business before the weekend came. She also feared that if she stayed another day she might never want to leave.

The sweet aroma of fresh-baked apple pie greeted her as

she entered the cozy, but noisy restaurant. She was surprised by the rambunctious crowd of young and old people sitting at the various wooden tables.

Michael waved to several of the ranchers who turned to greet him. He had forgotten how much he missed socializing with the friendly group that swarmed around him as he held a chair for Vanessa to sit down in the only empty table he could find.

"How's it goin', Mikey?" one old-timer called from across the room. Vanessa guessed he probably occupied that table most days, but was proven wrong as she listened to the continuing conversation.

"Not bad. Get many calves this year, Frank?" Michael asked, turning to prop his tanned forearm on the back of the chair to face the old rancher.

"Got me enough to keep me hoppin'," Frank said with a smile that showed years of neglect in his brown teeth.

Michael nodded at several others before turning back to face his guest. "Sorry, I forgot what this place was like," he apologized to a quiet Vanessa.

"Don't apologize. This is great. It smells wonderful, apple pie and cow dung," she whispered, so only he could hear.

His laughter rang out and Vanessa coloured slightly from the attention they were drawing. A pretty red-headed girl approached and handed them each a menu.

"I haven't seen you for a long time, Mr. Ryan."

Michael squinted his eyes at her, trying to place the pretty face with the upturned nose and bright blue eyes. "Oh, Sally, I hardly recognized you. You sure have grown up. How's your folks these days?"

They chatted idly for a few minutes as Vanessa watched in fascination. He seemed so at ease with all these people. Quite different than when she first saw him as he entered a room full of strangers. She had considered him arrogant and egotistical, but now she appreciated the chance to see the real man she was falling in love with. Sally gave her a genuine smile before quickly placing their orders with the cook.

The noise in the room subsided as the regulars finished their breaks from the everyday chores that were a given with ranching. There was always more to do, but by the look on all the faces, Vanessa guessed they were quite happy with the life of the rancher. She wondered if she could settle down to that kind of life.

Deep in thought, Michael fidgeted with his spoon. He drank his coffee black, but the fingers that soothed her last night needed something to touch, and Vanessa's straight shoulders and back were across the table from him. He watched her as she sipped her own black coffee.

His broad hand reached for her smooth one, gently stroking the long fingers. He hesitated, picking up her outstretched hand in his, and covered it with his other one.

"Vanessa," he started to say. Her eyes lifted from the coffee cup, glinting green in the afternoon sun that sparkled through the cafe curtains. "I would like you to live with me." There, he said it. The thin film of perspiration beaded his forehead.

Vanessa stared at the steel gray eyes that wouldn't allow her to look away. "Oh, Michael." She was at a loss for words, unsure if her feelings for him would be the right ones to follow. "I can't do that," she said, pulling her captured hand away to lift the steaming cup to her mouth with two shaking hands.

Michael followed suit. They stared over the rims of the coffee cups, each unsure of what to say next. The silence built a wall of awkwardness between them.

Vanessa thought about the dream she had last night. Did he actually say he loved her? It was too soon for that, she chided herself. No one falls in love this quickly, even if they are attracted to one another as she and Michael obviously were. "You were great last night, but I'm not about to start a relationship on the basis of great sex." She coloured deeply. Talking so frankly about a touchy subject was not one of her strong points. "We need to get to know each other a little more before I can even consider such an offer."

Michael nodded. A lump in his throat halted him from

telling her he wanted her to live with him the day he met her. He cursed himself silently for not thinking it through. To her he must appear like a man who has found a perfect lover and wants to keep her to himself. How could he be so crass?

They ate their meals in silence, each absorbed in thoughts of their own. Michael felt as if he had just been slapped in the face, and the sting of her words continued to ring in his ears. Vanessa, confused and annoyed with herself, struggled to fight back the tears that seemed so close to flowing right now. She knew she had to come to terms with her old relationship with Mark before she could start a new one. It was time to face the music, she thought, admit that Mark had not been the perfect man for her.

"We better be getting back now," he said, rising suddenly out of the wooden seat. He stuffed his hand into the tight jeans pocket and threw a couple of bills on the table for Sally.

Vanessa walked through the door as he held it open for her. He caught the subtle scent of her perfume, but was careful not to touch her for fear of scaring her off even more than she was already. He cursed himself silently as he climbed into his side of the Jeep.

They drove back in silence. A conversation would be fruitless over the drone of the tires on the road. Vanessa leaned back in the black leather seat and took in the beautiful countryside. She knew she had to leave tomorrow. It would be too late tonight. Besides she didn't want to be driving in the dark, she told herself. Or was it that she couldn't bear to leave him so soon? She hadn't told him that she loved him, and he didn't confess anything to her, either. How could she be sure unless he did? He didn't even tell her that he loved her, did he? Suddenly she was confused by what could have been a dream last night. Did he actually save her from the broken branch, tell her he loved her?

She felt the confusion clog her mind. He had been all she wanted last night, but still she couldn't bring herself to say yes to his proposal to live with him. Was she so much of a prude, she thought, that she wouldn't even consider living with a man, especially one she felt so much for? No, that was not it, or else she would never have allowed herself to fall prey to his seductive advances.

Her heart pounded the moment he shut off the engine, silencing the noise that separated them. She grabbed his wrist as he jerked the keys out of the ignition. They had to talk, right now.

"Michael, I need more than you wanting me to live with you. I need you to love me, to tell me you love me. To want to marry me."

He stared ahead for a few seconds before answering. "Vanessa, I'm afraid to tell you those things." His usual smile was replaced by a disturbing cloud of frustration. "If you lived with me, you would have the chance to leave if things didn't work out. I couldn't handle a second divorce." His face showed tiny lines around the beautiful gray eyes. She touched his hair, brushing it away from his warm forehead.

"I won't live with you, Michael, because I believe in commitment, and when I make that commitment, it's forever. This is hard to admit, and I've never told anyone," she said, taking a deep breath before continuing, "but if Mark hadn't died, I'd still be married to him even if he made my life miserable because that's just the way I was raised."

Michael's eyes widened in surprise. "Did he make your life miserable, Vanessa?" he asked, softly.

Vanessa turned away to hide the tears that welled up again. "Yes, he made me unhappy. There were things he said that hurt me and I could never understand why he would say them, but I still loved him. I would never have left him."

"But you can't compare your life with Mark to what we could have. You know that, don't you?" Michael hunched over the steering wheel as he stared intently at her.

"I know, I'm just terrified to try again, that's all. It's like you are just too good to be true!" Vanessa wiped her nose with the back of her hand. "Let's give ourselves some time," she reasoned. She was gifted with having a cool head, her mother always told her, but being around him was making it difficult not to take him up on his offer. She tried to think of the business to take her mind off telling him yes right now.

Michael walked around the front of the Jeep, stopping beside her door. Vanessa took a deep breath before stepping down, accepting the offer of his helping hand.

"Vanessa, I want you with me," he whispered, pulling her into his warmth as he surrounded her with his long arms.

"I know that, Michael, but I have a business to run, and so do you. I can't see this being any more than an affair," she blurted before she knew she was saying it.

"The business is just an excuse and you know it," Michael said, his voice raised in frustration. Michael exhaled loudly. "I don't know how I'm going to convince you that it is right for us to be together. But I won't force you to live with me." He stared intently at the deep pools of green that he had grown to adore.

"No, it's not, but it is something I am committed to and I intend to keep running it. No man is going to take that part of me away, too," she cried as she raced up the front steps.

Michael stood beside the Jeep, shaking his head sadly. If he was going to win her over to his side, he knew he had to exorcise the ghosts that haunted the beautiful woman who had waltzed into his heart.

In the kitchen, Vanessa leaned over the sink to run cold water for a drink. Something about watching Michael saunter up the walk stirred her uncontrollably. She had to decide what was more important to her, her work or her heart. She feared failing at either project, but at least the blame could be cast elsewhere in the business. It would be her fault if things didn't work out with Michael and she wasn't ready to face that possibility just yet.

Michael crossed over to her and touched her hair. The heat of his body as it touched her sparked the desire she had felt last night. She would stay one more night, she decided, and then, she would have to head home, or be caught up in the possibility of leaving everything she had worked for behind, just for a man. She wasn't ready to do that, not yet. She knew it.

The heat in the kitchen was almost unbearable. He threw open the window over the sink as Vanessa wandered into the living room. The sun was now on the back side of the house and the coolest place would be the living room and den. He poured two cold glasses of wine from the fridge before carrying them into the living room where Vanessa sat in silence.

The room was dark and quiet. She had not turned on the overhead light. He allowed his eyes to adjust to the dimness before finding her curled up on the couch.

"Are you okay? Here, drink this." He held the cold glass in his outstretched hand as he stood in front of her.

She looked up at the figure looming over her. "Thanks." She took a sip before placing it on the table beside her.

Michael made himself comfortable sitting cross-legged on the floor in front of her. He studied her for a moment before saying anything. "I'm sorry if I rushed you. I know you need time and space." His voice was soft, soothing her jumbled nerves. He had such an effect on her, making her feel out of control. It was not what she was used to.

She placed a finger to his lips to hush him. The pulsing blood in her veins quickened as he moved toward her. He placed his drink beside her, reaching across to rest it on the table. His chest grazed her breasts, making them tingle at his touch. She wrapped her sinewy arms around his shoulders, trapping him in her lap. She gently stroked his forehead, running her fingers through his hair, drawing circles around his temples.

"Keep that up, and you'll be sorry," he said, a sensual tone in his voice.

"No, I won't be 'sorry', as you so bluntly put it. I know I want you, and I only have one more night left." Her voice whispered in the darkness, enveloping him in its warmth.

Silence screamed in the overwhelming quiet. It was a moment before the realization of what she said sank in. His eyes widened and his mouth dropped.

She bent her head over his, lifting her knees up so she could kiss him full on the lips. He pulled her down with his strong arms, positioning her on top of him. She nestled down on his chest, pressing her cheek over his pounding heart.

He was determined to make the night last. This time he came prepared, but he wanted to get the mood just right, try to seduce her to see his way as the right one. He slid his rigid body out from under her, leaving her laying on her flat stomach. She pulled her arms up and crossed them under her chin to watch as he started a fire in the rock fireplace. In the dim glow from the kitchen window, he searched for the paper and matches. It started in an instant, flames licking the dark cavern. He tossed a few logs on, gave a few more pokes and it was perfect.

Vanessa watched his hunched shoulders, sleek, muscled back, and tight butt as he squatted in front of the fire.

He turned, still resting on his haunches, using the poker to reposition a log that had fallen forward on the grate. "You look distracted," he perceived, correctly.

"I hate the thought of leaving tomorrow. Your place here is so beautiful. I understand why you chose here over any of the cities you work in."

"Then why not stay? You could sell the business..." he started, unable to finish his thought as she jumped from the floor, eyes flashing.

"Sell the business?" Her sudden flare of indignation rose in her voice sending him sprawling on the floor, taken aback by her outburst. She quickly tried to regain her composure, aware of his steely glare searing into her. Her hands twisted in her lap, confused, unable to convey the annoyance she felt as she settled back onto the couch.

"Why should I? You of all people should know just how important that business is to me, how far I've come with it in four years. I can't just walk away from something like that." She stared incredulously at the statuesque pose he held in front of the roaring fire.

His even tone surprised him as he spoke, trying to conceal the hurt and anger that welled up inside. He had thought their time together had been special, something that comes only once in a lifetime. He could not believe she was going to throw it all away for a business, no matter how profitable it was. "Why don't you just think about it?" he asked quietly, meeting her eyes with a steady gaze.

"Maybe I'll just sleep on it," she retorted, as she stormed out of the cozy room, her face burning from the anger she felt. Why should she give up her business for him? He didn't even tell her he loved her. What if it didn't work out?

Vanessa slammed the guest room door, crumpling against it as she broke into tears. Damn him, anyway. Why did she not believe in her first impression of him? Why did she have to be so attracted to him? Is this what it was supposed to feel like to end an affair? That is exactly what they had, she thought, her head bent onto her arms as she hugged her knees.

Michael sat in front of the fire long after the last flickering flame burned out. The fire he had felt for her still raged inside, even though he had tried to douse it with the last of the wine he had opened for the abbreviated evening together. She was gone. Forever, now, he thought, rubbing his tired eyes with his thumb and forefinger.

After tending to Major, he slowly walked up the stairs, turning out the lights behind him. It was a long, sleepless night for him, tossing in the bed that had held their loving bodies just one night before.

Vanessa rose early Monday morning. Her eyes, puffy and swollen, glared back at her in the antique mirror. It was going to take a couple minutes with a cold cloth to try to get herself looking half decent. Silently she crept to the bathroom. It was only five in the morning, and the house was still silent. Good. She didn't feel like facing him just yet.

She couldn't shake the image of the dream she had last night. Their bodies were intertwined, lying in a field of daisies, the soft breeze cooling their heated skins. He was gentle and loving, all she ever wanted. His body was tanned and lean, his kisses soft and wet. His face hidden in the shadows. It wasn't Michael, she told herself. How could it be?

She tried to clear her head, as she leaned over the deep tub to turn on the faucets. She hoped the rush of water wouldn't disturb him at such an early hour, but she needed to cleanse her soul of the overwhelming desire to throw her career away and rush into his arms. But that was a foolish, romantic notion, one that only appeared under semi-conscious conditions.

Vanessa dried off quickly, wrapping the luxurious blue towel under her arms, tucking the top end in front to hold it in place. She opened the door.

"Whoa, not so fast," he said, grabbing her upper arms to prevent her from forcing her way around him.

"I've got to get…" was all she said before his mouth covered hers with a hard, determined kiss. She felt herself melt, but quickly recovered when the image of last night's disagreement returned.

"Good morning, beautiful," he said. Releasing his grip, he stepped back to admire the shapely outline of the fluffy towel. "I'll be down in a minute to start breakfast," he said.

"I'll get dressed," she said quietly, skirting his appreciative look as she ducked her head to walk under the outstretched arms that held the door frame of the tiny room.

She could hear the muffled sounds of the man's footsteps as she closed the door behind him. Her face was burning. Why did she let him get under her skin like that? Life was going so smoothly until she took that damned seminar. Why couldn't she have been happy with the business the way it was? If she hadn't signed up for it, she would have missed the opportunity to have met Michael, she knew, but maybe it was fate that planned things that way. After all, she had been to other lectures before, and not fallen madly in love with the instructors. Thank goodness, she thought, remembering some of the ones she had encountered.

She busied herself getting dressed and packing her things into the open suitcase. The thought of leaving brought an unexplained pang of sadness, one that stabbed at her heart unexpectedly. Was she throwing it all away, just to return to the admittedly boring life she had been leading these past few years? Or was she running away from it, scared to accept the challenge of finding a new life?

She ended up wearing a clean pair of navy slacks, and a cream silk blouse. That darn dog better not be downstairs, she thought as she lifted the heavy suitcase off the bed.

She struggled to the bottom of the stairs with her load, depositing it at the entrance to the living room. She didn't dare look inside the warm, rustic room. The reminder of the roaring fire he had started for them was only cause for more guilt. She had enough to contend with now, she thought, as she walked slowly into the kitchen.

Vanessa flicked on the light as she entered. Even at six in the morning the room had a homey feeling. She sighed deeply, feeling as if she had already lost a friend. She felt as if she'd had enough of living alone, and the emptiness that tugged at her heart as she started the coffee settled within her. Tonight she would be dining alone. She chased away the thought with a swipe at her eyes with her free hand. The hot tears escaped the rough gesture. She shuffled across the room and plopped down in the waiting chair.

She could hear his heavy footsteps on the stairs. She tensed, unwilling to face him but knowing she must. She forced a smile as his looming figure filled the doorway.

"Seems I'm always apologizing for my actions," Michael said, running a strong hand through his hair. Vanessa warmed inside at the memory of those capable hands on her body. They didn't move from their places, but Vanessa had to picture herself glued to her chair in an effort not to rush into his arms.

"It's me who should apologize," she said. He watched in silence. She swallowed and continued, folding her hands in front of her on the clean table. "I can imagine what you thought when I…responded to you so strongly. I need the time to sort out how I feel, see what I'm going to do with my life."

"You already said that," he answered, flatly. "What I need is you to be with me, to live with me, but we already know that answer, don't we?" He gave a sad smile, and it pulled at Vanessa's heart not to give him the answer he craved. She knew she wasn't ready, he had to understand. She watched him closely with guarded emotions.

"Give me a month," she said, quietly as she lowered her eyes. The sting from the unshed tears burned her eyes. She rose from her seat and brushed past him. The fire in his eyes burned into hers as she looked at him before heading into the living room to retrieve her bags.

Silently he watched her as she struggled with her load to the little sports car that was parked on the grass in front of the house. His heart fell when he realized she wouldn't look back.

Seven

The eerie silence of the morning crept into the tidy office where Vanessa sat, rolling the yellow pencil between her palms. It was only eight and Janice wasn't due to arrive until nine. That gave her an hour of solitude, something she felt she needed, knowing she had to make a decision about the business, and Michael.

It had been a long drive yesterday through Tete Jaune and along the Yellowhead Highway to Prince George. She had a quick coffee and muffin at the Sandman Inn in McBride. The serenity of the rolling hills that sharply peaked into mountains did not do much in the way of calming her agitated mind.

She had concentrated on her driving to keep her thoughts from wandering back to the gentler times spent with Michael.

She decided she had to put him in the past if she was going to get on with running her life. It was an affair, and although it was sweet, it was over. They could never make it work, she thought, knowing how much time he spent away from home doing his seminars. That would be the same as Mark being on the road so much, she thought, remembering how she hated the lonely nights.

She reached for a blank yellow legal pad and drew a line down the middle. On one side she wrote pros, and on the other, cons and started to think about the future.

Under the cons she wrote Michael, no time together. Under the pros she listed the company, the people, the incentive program, stability. She underlined Michael, and wrote love, security, outdoors. But would there be security, she wondered, recalling that he said that if she lived with him, she could move out if things didn't work out. Why did he have to worry about a divorce if he truly loved her? The thought gnawed at her for the next half hour while she sat back in the big leather chair, staring at the couch that he had sat on the first time he had visited her office.

He certainly had a way of eating into her everyday existence, she noted with frustration. She hadn't been back for twenty-four hours yet. She had to give herself time. Ever since that first night, and every waking moment since, her mind would wander back to thoughts of him. Did she have the same effect on him? Would she have an answer in a month? At the rate she was going, she'd be lucky if she could come to a decision in a year, she thought, slamming the pencil down on the nearly empty pad.

The soft knock on her half-open door forced her to look up. Janice poked her dark head in, a cheery smile that Vanessa found offensive to her dark mood flashed across her friend's face.

"Well, how was the holiday?" she asked, plopping herself down on the couch, waiting expectantly for all the details.

Vanessa greeted her with mixed emotions. "You told me to go get 'em, tiger, so I blame you for the mess I'm in." She made little effort to hide the frown that crossed her brow.

"Me?" Janice retorted. "What did I do? Better yet, what did you do?" she asked, leaning forward in her seat, eyes widening in anticipation.

"I did what you said. Only things are more complicated now." She sighed, resting her chin in her interlocked fingers. She proceeded to tell her friend and confidante most of what took place the short while she was gone. She left out how she really felt about him, since she was not sure herself.

"Looks like you have a big decision ahead," Janice said. "I wish I had the same problem," she teased, trying to pull her friend out of her melancholy mood.

"Yeah, I guess," Vanessa said, absently. "Tell me how things have been around here." That finished the small talk, allowing the two of them to discuss the future plans Vanessa intended to develop regarding the incentive program. Janice was sure it would be well received, and urged her to set it up as soon as possible.

"I'm also looking for a new warehouse for distributing the imports. You're from Victoria. What do you think about that city for a location?" Vanessa asked.

"That is an excellent idea. The new store there is doing very well, did I tell you? They had a fantastic week. That fellow you hired sounded so thrilled when he called to tell you what happened. What's his name?" Janice puckered her neat eyebrows into a disturbed frown. "Oh, Jason somebody. That guy loves to talk. I think he got my whole life story when he called. Don't be shocked when you see the phone bill," she added, chuckling softly.

"Jason Sanders. I hired him six months ago. It's almost time to fly down and see how he's doing." She made a mental note to call him later and make arrangements. "Would you make arrangements for me to be there on Friday? I'd like to spend the weekend on the island."

She watched as Janice nodded, a somber expression clouded her friend's face. "Make that two tickets. You're coming with me."

Janice flashed a bright smile before hurrying out the door to make reservations before Vanessa had a chance to reconsider.

Janice could show her the sights in Victoria. Maybe a small escape away from the thoughts of Michael would help. Living in British Columbia for over half her life, Vanessa had never seen the Parliament Buildings, the Empress Hotel, the Victoria harbour that was so picturesque.

The rest of the week flew by. Vanessa immersed herself in the business at hand, arranging for the financial department to set up the incentive program, looking over the possibility of buying a warehouse in Victoria, instead of the one they presently leased in Vancouver. She contacted Jason on Thursday to inform him of her plans personally.

"I've already spoken to Janice," he said, cheerfully. "I'm looking forward to your visit. Everything is set up for you. I've got a warehouse all lined up for you to look at when you get here. The guy seems anxious to sell. I guess it's been costing him a fortune leaving it empty. I think you could get it for a steal." The excitement in Jason's voice helped raise her spirits. At least someone was in a good mood, she thought, trying to shake the depression she had fallen into since her return.

Vanessa hung up, thinking she detected something different in Jason's voice. Maybe it was just more confidence in his work now that he had been working for her for six months. But she knew that was not it. She had hired him because he was smart, and had a cockiness about him that she felt was a plus in starting the business on the island. She needed someone who was very sure of himself and aggressive. He seemed more cheerful, that was all she could think of. Anyway, it would be a profitable visit she was sure.

Janice chatted for the entire flight to Vancouver. The only rest Vanessa had was the stopover in Vancouver when she took advantage of the spare time to call the other stores on the lower mainland.

It was different having the head office in Prince George,

and she was considering looking into putting a tie line to the Vancouver stores, to cut down on the telephone charges. There seemed to be so much work to do with the company growing so quickly. Even the stores in Alberta should be connected. She'd have to start on that project as soon as she got back, she thought, as she hung up on her final call.

"That was our call for boarding, Vanessa," Janice said, breathlessly, as she grabbed her boss's arm and guided her through the enclosed walkway to the aircraft. "Good thing you brought me along," she chided.

Vanessa laughed. "I'm beginning to think the same thing." When they were seated, Vanessa described her plans for a telephone system that they needed to work on.

"Why don't you let me take care of that for you? My brother works for BCTel in the sales division. I'm sure he could help us out."

"Great. That's one less thing to worry about." Vanessa glanced out the window as they flew over the water between Vancouver Island and the mainland.

"You sure you're okay? I mean, you look awfully stressed out this week," Janice said, concern for her friend etched visibly on her plain, but not unattractive face. "We're going to have to relax this weekend, after the visit, that is."

Vanessa nodded, placing her briefcase under the seat in front of her, and settled back to enjoy the view. It was a short flight and Jason was there to greet them and take them directly to the store. Vanessa relaxed in the back seat, allowing Janice and Jason to chat all they wanted up front. They seemed made for each other, Vanessa thought. She smiled silently to herself. Neither of them stopped talking long enough for her to have to say anything, which was fine with her.

Jason introduced them to his staff, and showed her the improvements he had made in the store since she last visited. Vanessa was pleased with his work and complimented him and his staff on the increase in the sales and the look of the store.

It was almost noon when they reached the hotel. Jason had

booked the Empress the moment he was informed of their plans to visit. The three of them ate a delicious lunch in the elegant, understated luxury of the Empress's dining room before Vanessa and Jason headed to the site of the warehouse.

Janice opted to wander along the harbour, walking to the Wax Museum and exploring the tiny shops along the busy streets. When Janice returned, she found Vanessa seated in the lobby reading the newspaper. Vanessa noted her friend was flushed from the walk and the warmth of the sunny day as she rose to greet Janice in the lobby of the Empress.

"I'll just relax in my room tonight," Janice said over tea. She pushed her sweaty bangs off her forehead. Her cheeks reflected the pink in her damp blouse.

Vanessa laughed. "Sorry, kiddo. If I knew where there was a flower shop I'd be sending tiger lilies to you."

Janice's puzzled expression prompted Vanessa to continue.

"I had to explain to Jason that you didn't come with me because of business but because you wanted to see Victoria again and left me to do business. You should have seen the pouty expression he tried to hide. Anyway, you better get cleaned up because I told him you would love to take a horse and buggy ride up to Beacon Hill Park this evening, after dinner." Vanessa couldn't hide the smug expression from her incredulous friend.

"You did what?" Janice asked, brown eyes wide in astonishment. "You can't leave me alone with him. I hardly know him." Her hand shook as the cup tinkled, hitting the delicate china saucer.

"How long did I know Michael? Besides, I spent time alone with him and you weren't worried on my account," Vanessa teased. "You told me to go get 'em, remember? Now it's your turn." Vanessa enjoyed matching them up, even though she was still unsure of her own match with Michael.

""You should have asked me first," Janice started, but the look on Vanessa's face indicated she was already licked. "I guess I better get started then." Janice pushed her chair away, leaving Vanessa smiling in her wake.

Vanessa finished the last of her tea before heading to her own elegantly decorated room to retire for the evening. It had been a very productive day. Jason's ideas were certainly worth considering and she wanted to jot them down so she could think each one over. Moving the head office to Victoria was one of the best ones he had come up with, and she couldn't find any reason not to, except the fact that she would have to move herself.

There really wasn't anyone she would miss in Prince George, she thought as she opened the tapestry suitcase she had left on her bed when they checked in. There wasn't anyone at all in her life, she thought, sinking onto the hard bed in the suddenly dreary room. She dug through the few outfits she hadn't had a chance to unpack. She found the nightie she had taken to Blue River, wondering why she had brought it. There was no Michael here to wear it for.

Hot tears pushed their way down her cheeks as she fought the loneliness that had been overwhelming her ever since her hasty return from the ranch. Annoyance at Michael for suggesting she sell the business changed to longing to feel his body pressed against hers, legs entwined in an intimate embrace.

Vanessa brushed out the French braid she had worn all day, trying to forget the feel of Michael's hands running through her hair. The relaxing soak in the deep tub only made her long to hear his voice, feel his touch. She slipped into the nightie she had never had a chance for him to see. It was just an affair. She might never hear from him again, she thought, overcome with a sadness that made her feel more lonely than she ever felt in her life.

She still had his number in her purse, but she stopped herself from dialing. What was she going to tell him, anyway? She had said she would have an answer in one month. Already a week had slipped by and she was no closer to an answer. Her heart told her to go to him, be with him. But her mind still struggled with the little voice that told her not to give up what she had—the business Mark had nurtured, the certainty and security of the business. She couldn't become a kept woman again. Michael hadn't asked her to marry him, she reminded herself. She would just be the woman who lived with him. She couldn't do that. She needed his commitment for life.

She climbed into the empty bed, acutely aware of the need for male companionship, and love.

Vanessa was awakened by the ringing of the phone next to her ear as she lay clutching the hard pillow against her chest. She rubbed her eyes sleepily as she stretched to reach the annoyance.

"Hello," she answered, sleepily.

"Hi," the husky voice responded. "Did I wake you?"

Vanessa sat up, eyes flying open. "Where are you?" she asked, recognizing Michael's voice instantly.

"I'm in Vancouver. I'm doing a seminar here. I called your office and they told me where you were."

"Oh," she said, pulling the pillow up behind her to sit up in the bed.

"I didn't know you were planning another trip," he said, a hint of annoyance reflected in his voice.

"I don't have to tell you what I'm doing. It's my business, and I do what I see fit." Anger slowly boiled within her. He had no right to know what she was doing in her business.

He sensed her defensiveness. He quickly changed the subject. "Did you have a pleasant drive home?"

Vanessa cringed at the thought of how she had walked out that morning. "Yes," she said.

The silence hung on the wire between them.

"When are you finished?" Vanessa ventured, her voice quivering at the possibility of seeing him again.

"It's just for this afternoon. I was going to head back tomorrow. I thought, maybe, well..." It wasn't like him to be at a loss for words, but the fear that she may not want to see him again hung in the air. He was crazy with the desire to see her.

"I'm finished here. Janice and I were going to tour the island for the rest of the weekend, but I think she might have changed her mind," she said, glancing at her watch as it lay on the night stand. Vanessa remembered Janice's vow to get her up at seven and it was already nine in the morning.

"Why don't you fly over here and we can have an evening together before we each head home?" He held his breath, not wanting to force himself on her, but needing her to say yes.

Vanessa hesitated, wanting to see him, but fearful that things could get out of hand. After all, it was just an affair, she reminded herself. She shouldn't be getting tied up with him at his every whim. Still, she couldn't overcome the need to see him.

"Where will I find you?" she asked, reaching for the note pad she had scribbled on the night before.

"I'll meet you at the airport. When can you get in?"

"I'll be on the afternoon flight. I'll make arrangements now. Where can I reach you if the flight is booked?"

He gave her his room number, and told her to leave a message at the desk, as the seminar was in the same hotel. They chatted for a few more minutes before saying goodbye.

Vanessa replaced the receiver on the phone, holding her hand over it for a few seconds, wondering if she was doing the right thing. Should she call back and cancel? It frightened her that she could need him so much, yet a glimmer of hope flitted through her, making her insides glow with anticipation.

She rang Janice's room. They made arrangements to meet for breakfast in half an hour. Vanessa checked over what was left to wear, deciding on the green silk blouse and cream pants. After a quick shower, she braided her hair back off her face, tying it with a neat bow of cream lace at the nape of her neck. She was starting to have a bit of a healthy glow after the few days on the ranch and the time spent outside in Victoria. She used a little bit of mascara and glossed her lips with a natural shade, and added a touch of blush before packing up all her toiletries into the travel bag. She was placing the last of her clothes in the suitcase when the soft rapping sounded from the door.

She greeted the smiling face as she held the door open for Janice to walk in. "I just have to gather my purse," she said, noting the pink tones in Janice's face that weren't there yesterday morning.

"You look great," Vanessa commented, closing the locked door behind her.

Janice coloured from the open neck of her white blouse to the roots of the dark brown hair she kept tied back in a shoulder length bob. "Don't tease me, or I won't tell you anything about last night."

They laughed as they passed a tourist couple on the stairs leading to the dining room. They waited until they were seated to continue with the details of Janice's date with Jason.

"He's so sweet," she said, sipping the orange juice placed in front of her almost immediately after their orders were taken. Vanessa watched with keen interest, acutely aware that Janice was captivated by a man she had met only yesterday. She knew it was possible, thinking about Michael as she took a sip of the hot black coffee.

"I knew you two would hit it off," Vanessa said, smugly. "What have you got planned for today?" she asked, opening the burgundy napkin and placing it on her lap.

The sound of the fork as it clinked against the plate before falling onto the carpeted flooring ricocheted in the bustling room. Janice blushed, swearing softly under her breath.

"Don't tell me. You forgot we were going to Butchart Gardens." Vanessa's laughter filled the room. She was unaware of the eyes turned to stare at the two of them. She reached over and touched Janice's hand which was nervously twisting the napkin between her fingers.

"Yes," she said self-consciously, "I did. I'll call Jason and tell him I can't…"

"You'll do no such thing. I'm glad you made plans without including me." She proceeded to tell her about the call from Michael and that she was going to meet him this afternoon.

"That's wonderful. I hope you have a good time."

Vanessa looked down at the untouched toast on the delicate china plate. "I'm going to tell him I can't live with him. I still love the business and there's so much to do…"

"Vanessa, I think you're making a mistake. Don't lose him," she warned, her brown eyes flashing. "Business is not the most important thing in life. I wish you'd realize that."

"Those are pretty powerful statements coming from someone who makes a living from my business." Vanessa stared at Janice, each trying to hold back the smiles that were playing at the corners of their mouths.

"I could always come and work for Jason," Janice teased. "Then I would have a boss who wouldn't be such a slave-driver."

Vanessa almost choked on her coffee, as the laughter spilled from her mouth. "I swear, that man Jason has made you as cocky as he is, and only in one day." Janice glowed brightly.

"Well, you should know the effect a good man can have on a woman. If Michael has any sense, he'd find a way to make you come around to his way of thinking, just like Jason." She smiled at her friend, before rising to start her day with her new-found friend. "See you back home. Have a nice evening," she added, giving Vanessa a mischievous wink. This time it was Vanessa's turn to blush.

The rest of the morning dragged as Vanessa strolled along the dock, watching the ships pass or enter the beautiful harbour in the warm sunshine. She thought about what she was going to tell Michael, but the answer was not within her grasp.

Jason had her charged up to move the head office to Victoria, and she was eager to start on the analysis of the proposal. It didn't matter where her head office was situated in the sense that she could get all the information from the company stores from her main computer, which could be set up anywhere. Victoria made more sense if she was going to go ahead with the phone system, linking all the stores to a more central location. And having the warehouse right there was an added plus. It was time she made the move, especially with the expansion she was planning in the next few years. Prince George was just too far away from most of the stores. It could serve as a base for any stores that she put in Edmonton, or Prince Albert, but for now, she decided to concentrate on expanding to the east, not north.

• • •

The tiled floor of the airport corridor was jammed with people heading both ways. Vanessa, carrying her tote bag and purse, was jostled in the crowd. She barely glanced out the tinted windows that ran from the departure gate to the waiting rooms. It was humid, at least thirty degrees, and a tiny trickle of perspiration ran down her back.

Vanessa slowed, unsure of which area to stand to wait for her suitcase. There were two conveyor belts spewing out baggage, allowing the unclaimed pieces to circle on the belt until all the passengers arrived. She read the sign that announced the airline she had flown and she walked up to it, spying her tapestry case as she peered over some Japanese tourists who moved aside politely, smiling appreciatively at her tall, neatly tailored appearance.

After retrieving her bag, she turned to scan the area that held anyone who had not just arrived from entering the baggage area. Michael was there, tall and tan, leaning against the waist high railing, smiling at her. Her heart beat faster. Her palms moistened as she carried her burden to the lobby, dropping the case beside her as he pulled her close, surprising her with a welcome kiss.

"Michael, I..." She tried to speak, but the sudden press of his warm, wet lips extinguished her words.

She felt his strong hand against the back of her head. She returned his kiss with burning lips as she melted in his warm embrace, unaware of the stares they were receiving, as they blocked the exit from the baggage area. A portly man cleared his throat loudly, pushing his girth against her hips.

"We better move over," she whispered. Michael picked her case up in an easy gesture, and wrapped his arm around her shoulder as he continued to stare at the intense green eyes that held his. He guided her out the main doors, leading her to the parking lot. The warm air hit her in the face, making her gasp. The line up of taxi cabs with their engines running expelled fumes that settled under the heat of the afternoon.

"I parked my car over here," he said, guiding her down the

narrow cement steps to the parking lot.

"I thought you drove a Jeep," she said, looking up into the beautiful gray eyes she had missed so much.

"I keep an old beater parked here most of the time. It's a lot cheaper than renting one every time I fly in here. Here we are," he said, finding his keys in his suit pocket.

Vanessa stepped aside to allow him to open the door to the late model Camaro, but before she could get in, he trapped her against the hot side of the red vehicle, his weight pressed against her as she returned his hot, moist kisses, his mustache tickling her sensitive neck and jaw.

His strong hands glided over her neatly tied hair, caressed her silky nape before exploring the smooth length of her back. Vanessa moaned with pleasure, forgetting her thoughts of ending the affair, that it would not be worth pursuing. Just having him touch her again sent shivers of delight racing through her veins. His arms held her tightly, his body pressed into hers with an urgency she mirrored with her own aching body.

"I missed you," he whispered, his breath hot against her ear. His hands held her face, as he gently tilted her chin upward, forcing her to admit her desire by meeting his penetrating gray eyes with her own wide green ones.

"Michael, I missed you, too." She ran her hands through his hair, making him groan deeply in his throat. He released her quickly, placing her suddenly in the cooling vehicle and closed her door. If they didn't get out of the lot fast, he knew they could be arrested for what he wanted to do next.

Vanessa's flushed cheeks burned as he touched her once more before starting the engine. It roared loudly as he stepped on the gas, swerving expertly into the rush hour traffic. She watched him as he shifted into gear, racing toward the city center of downtown Vancouver.

"Where are we going?" she asked, turning sideways to drink in the full aroma of maleness sitting next to her. He was wearing the same intoxicating scent, she remembered, the day she met him. She wondered if that is what triggered her response to him earlier. No, it was the man, himself, who evoked her reaction.

"I wanted to surprise you and book a flight to someplace exotic and secluded, to fly away never to return," he teased, smiling at her with his crazy upturned grin.

"Why didn't you?" she challenged, wondering what it would be like to be kidnapped by someone so powerfully attractive.

"I couldn't wait the length of the flight to be with you." His gray eyes betrayed the pent-up desire trapped deep within the man she loved.

They drove for a short distance, following the traffic leading into the downtown core. He turned the car into the underground parking lot of the hotel he was booked into earlier.

"I thought you said your seminar ended this afternoon," she said, standing to the side of the door as he flung it open.

"I did. I booked a room for another night after I called you." He bent his head to kiss her again on the lips, holding her close in the dark parking lot. He led her through the lobby, carrying her bag in one hand while his other one held her closely by the waist as they headed for the elevator.

The door was almost closed when Michael dropped the suitcase and pressed the button for the ninth floor. Turning to her, he lifted her face to gently kiss her soft, waiting mouth. One strong hand captured her jaw as the other reached the small of her back to pull her against him. The ride was shorter than either would have liked, opening suddenly on the re-quired floor, forcing them apart as the cool draft shot through the door, indicating they had reached their destination.

He reached for her hand instinctively as they stepped out into the dimly lit hallway, neatly decorated with teal carpet and rose walls. Vanessa's heart pounded with anticipation as she waited behind him as he struggled for an instant with the electronic key.

The heavy door swung open with the ease of a paper airplane projected into a dull classroom. The room carried the elegance of the hotel through to the elaborate bathroom, complete with jacuzzi, Vanessa noticed, stepping inside.

She watched him as he closed the rose curtains to block out the afternoon sun which filtered through the open window. She did not move from her place just inside the door. Her suitcase was sitting neatly in the open closet. She hadn't noticed him place it out of her way.

Vanessa sucked in her breath, feeling the heat of the room rise several degrees instantly as she watched him remove his suit jacket and toss it on the bed. He struggled with the tie for a moment before throwing it aside. She stood motionless, drinking in the splendid beauty of his upper body wrapped in a crisp white shirt, which only enhanced the tan that had darkened significantly since she saw him last. He closed the door behind her as he gently placed his hand on her forearm.

"Let me look at you. It's only been one week, but I have to tell you it was a miserable, lonely week." He peered into the wide green pools that had haunted him at night. The green silk blouse only served to emphasize the resemblance her eyes held to the emeralds he had admired on his grandmother. His eyes followed the length of her throat, the open V at her neck, the softly rising silk of her blouse as it flowed over her breasts.

Vanessa followed his gaze, warming instantly as his touch ran the length of her silk-covered arms.

"Reservations are made, but not until seven-thirty," he said, dropping his arms to his sides and stepping back. "We have about two hours to kill." His eyes stared intently at her, conveying silently how he'd like to spend the rest of the afternoon.

"It's so warm, why don't we find a cool spot somewhere," she suggested, fearing that if they stayed too long in the heated room, they would not want to leave. She was also undecided about how far she was going to let the relationship develop.

A flash of fury crossed his face, making her step back quickly, hitting the door with a loud thump.

"You agree to meet me at the airport, follow me willingly up to this room, then suggest we go out to find a cool spot somewhere," he barked, grabbing her arm to pull her into view of his hostile stare.

She struggled to free her arm that hurt suddenly from the pressure he placed on it. "I can do what I damn well please," she retorted, "but that doesn't mean I don't want to stay here with you." Her eyes flashed back at him, making him retreat a step.

"Then what is it that you want, Vanessa? Me? Or just the thought of me?" His anger at her reaction upset her. "You're going to have to make up your mind."

"I'm not sure I know you well enough yet. You certainly seem to get upset quickly when things don't go your way. You said I have a month. It's only been one week. If you want to call off your stupid deal, then fine, and I'll leave right now. You called to say we could spend an evening together, and right now, I couldn't tell you what it is I want. I don't know myself." She slumped against the door, too exhausted to fight him anymore.

"I get frustrated sometimes, Vanessa. I know I want you, but I'm afraid I could lose you if I make the wrong move. I find it hard to control my emotions when you are around." He stood facing her, hands tucked into his pants pockets. His boyish appearance warmed Vanessa's heart as she smiled.

"I know. It frustrates me too. I've lived too long by myself, become self-sufficient and I enjoy being able to do as I please. I've asked you already to be patient and give me time." Vanessa stood waiting by the door, unsure of his next move, but not ready to relinquish any power in their situation. She had to hold her ground or she would be lost in another man's world once more. She knew that wasn't what she wanted.

He retrieved his tie and jacket. Vanessa watched him replacing the tie with quick, jerking motions as he stood in front of the mirror, crouching a bit to get the full view. "I know a perfect spot, if you'd like some quiet, too," he said, closing the door behind them. They walked in silence, careful not to touch each other as they headed to the car.

The short drive in the air-conditioned car cooled the

temper that flared in both of them. Michael's mood changed as quickly as he drove. The drive brought them to a riding stable on the outskirts of the city. Michael laughed at Vanessa's surprised look, indicating they certainly weren't dressed for a walk through the stables.

"Wait until we get inside."

Vanessa was astounded to find a quiet, neatly kept bar, with a few patrons milling around the television in the corner of the room, just off to one side. She strained to hear the familiar roar of a baseball game, but was surprisingly pleased when she discovered it was the tape of one of the most recent horse races held at the arena.

Michael filled her in on the history of the arena, and how he came to discover the place. She listened intently as he told how his horse, Danny Boy, was raised here, but had to be sold because of an injury in his very first race. He would have been a contender for one of the major races in the U.S. if he hadn't had the accident. She watched in fascination, noting the names of the horses who had been huge money winners in their days, their pictures proudly displayed on the oak wall surrounding the bar.

Taking a table that overlooked the indoor training arena, Michael held a chair for Vanessa. She smiled then directed her attention to the scene below. The glass prohibited them from hearing the coaching that was being given to a young rider from the sidelines where his coach stood, waving his arms.

"I used to ride like that," Vanessa admitted. Michael could not suppress the surprised look as she continued. "My parents sent me to a riding school every summer until I turned sixteen. I really quite enjoyed it."

"Why did you stop?"

"We couldn't afford it anymore. My father had a bad year on the farm, things just didn't work out. I always dreamed of owning my own horse someday, but, things change," she added, shrugging.

"That explains it," he said taking the last swig of the cold draft.

"Explains what?"

"The way you handled Rusty. Such grace and ease. Like a trained professional."

Vanessa blushed at the compliment. That was a week ago, and he still spoke with pride in his voice. She loved him, she knew, but he still hadn't brought up the subject of marriage, and she was not about to force him. She sat quietly sipping her drink, watching the young rider do the course with accomplished ease. She wondered how old the rider was.

"Do you know who he is?" Vanessa asked, pointing in the direction of the arena.

"I think that's the son of one of the owners here. Most of the kids ride. That's why their parents built this place."

"Hey, hey, wadaya know, Mikey's back." The scratchy voice came from behind them, followed quickly by a big, outstretched hand joining the tanned, muscular arm that slapped Michael on the back, making him tip his mug of beer precariously, but he managed to keep it upright.

"Well, if it isn't Jake McKenzie." Michael made the introductions, beckoning his old friend to join them. Vanessa sat back, quietly listening to the conversation.

"So, did you start that horse ranch you said you were going to?" Jake asked, settling back on the wooden chair, rocking dangerously on the back legs.

"No," Michael admitted, "there just doesn't seem to be the time. I'm pretty busy keeping the consulting business going. But I've still got old Danny Boy."

"Better let him sire a colt, put you back into the races. We miss you around here."

Vanessa watched, impressed by the knowledge he held about horses and the racing community in general. Michael's eyes betrayed the fact that he missed the track too. Vanessa smiled as he caught her eye, just as Jake rose to leave.

The men exchanged goodbyes as the three of them departed from the cozy little bar.

Eight

"Sell the business and live on the ranch with me." His cool gray eyes were almost black in the dim light of the elegant dining room. They had arrived in time for their reservations, getting their table almost immediately in the busy restaurant.

Vanessa shifted uncomfortably in her seat. She had to tell him exactly how she felt, even if it meant losing him if he was not in agreement to what she had to say. She swallowed the sip of wine she used to wet her unusually dry throat.

"Michael, I told you that my business is my life. I just can't become a fixture around a man's house again. I need the stimulation I get from work. If I lived with you on the ranch, what would I be doing? Tell me," she demanded. She held her breath, watching him as he stared intently at the plate of lobster in front of him.

"Would it make a difference if I told you that I loved you? That I want you to marry me?" he asked, his voice lowered almost to a whisper.

"If that is a proposal, it is the most pitiful one I have ever heard, Michael Ryan." She met his eyes with a cool gaze. "It makes a difference to me if you say you love me, but I have to know you mean it, and it still doesn't make me any less adamant about keeping busy with my work. I can't go back to being Mrs. Somebody or other. I'm me, and I love what I do. Can't you see that?"

His dark eyes flashed as he glanced up from his meal. "What am I supposed to do, Vanessa? I love you, and I want you with me. You know how I feel about marriage and if it doesn't work out. There's got to be a way to make this work for us." His eyes held hers, fire and passion filling his voice. He longed to hold her in his arms and make everything work out. But she was her own boss, he knew that, and it would take more than a night of passion to make her see his way.

"Let's not fight about it," she said, wearily. "I have a long day ahead of me tomorrow. Maybe we can both try to find a solution to our problem." She smiled, reaching for the strong hand that rested on the table beside his plate.

His steel eyes bored into her for a moment longer. She held his stare, fighting an invisible battle that raged between them. He quickly changed the subject, focusing on how her progress with the incentive program was coming. Her eyes lit up, full of enthusiasm, proud of the response her people were giving it. His heart sank as he realized he was number two in her life at this point in time.

The misty rain caressed their faces as they strolled along the damp sidewalk, his arm wrapped protectively around her shoulder, hers slipped behind his back. They walked in silence from the restaurant to the hotel where they had left the car after returning from the track.

Vanessa hugged him closer, breathing in his masculine scent gently mixed with the refreshing smell of rain. The hotel lobby was dark when they entered. It was after eleven already. They had passed more than three hours in the cozy restaurant, discussing horses and ranching, business and world events.

"I'll walk you to your room," he said, guiding her gently to the elevator in the middle of the lobby. The brass doors gleamed even in the semi-darkness of the night.

Vanessa tried to hide the hurt expression when she realized he planned to leave her alone tonight. The evening had been very intimate, except for the touchy discussion about her selling the business and living with him. She ached for him, thought he had realized her need. She was bitterly disappointed, riding silently in the quiet elevator.

"I'll just gather my things and book into another suite," he said, pushing the door open, leaving her to follow him in.

"Sure you don't want to stay for the night?" she heard her voice ask softly. She never envisioned herself as a seductress, but she tried her best with an inviting pose against the door.

"Sure you want me to? You won't have anyplace to escape to if I try anything," he said, staring intently into her warm green eyes. She responded by pushing the door closed with her back and locking it before walking over to where he stood in the center of the room, wrapping her sinewy arms around his neck, pulling him closer to her.

"Try everything you want," she whispered, her breath hot against his ear.

He gathered her up in a single swoop and dropped her gently onto the bed. She watched with heated anticipation as he tore the tie from around his neck, and reached to unbutton his collar.

"Let me do that," she said, rising onto her knees to meet him where he stood at the end of the bed. Her hot fingers worked diligently at the dozen buttons that separated his heated body from her own covered one. She pulled the white cotton shirt out of its captivity in the well-fitted trousers.

Michael shivered as she ran her tongue the length of his chest starting at his navel and working her way up. She slid the shirt off his muscular shoulders, running her hands across his back, pulling him onto the bed, his hands trapped in the buttoned cuffs of the now inside-out shirt.

"Wait, my cuffs…"

She smiled, a sultry smile he had never seen before. He ripped his hands out of their confinement, tossing the shirt aside as he engulfed her in a hungry embrace.

"Oh, Michael," she whispered, her head tossed back as he nuzzled her neck, unbuttoning her silk blouse with his free hand. She moaned as he ran his hands over her back and down the length of her sides, making her quiver inside.

He pulled away from her, trying to gain control of the situation. She was moving faster than he expected, and he wanted the evening to last.

"Why don't you start the jacuzzi, while I order something from room service?" he suggested, pulling away.

"But, Michael," she pleaded, wanting him more than she realized.

"Please, Vanessa." His gray eyes softened as he traced the line of her delicate jaw with his forefinger.

She obeyed, confused by his sudden halt to her advances.

"I'll be right back," he called through the closed bathroom door. "I have to get something downstairs." He buttoned his shirt quickly as he headed out the door.

After starting the water in the jacuzzi, Vanessa took the opportunity to change into the silky nightgown she had brought with her, reveling in its silky feel caressing her gently curved hips as she brushed out the braid that had held her blonde tresses for the entire day. The softness brushing across her bare back and shoulders felt good.

Michael returned quickly from the trip to his car. In one hand, he held the tiny gold-wrapped box, tied neatly with a gold bow. He smiled to himself as he remembered the clerk, a pretty redhead, eager to please him. She had painstakingly wrapped the gift as if it was for someone she loved, her delicate fingers arranging the strands of ribbon perfectly as she tied the intricate bow. He pictured the look on the clerk's face had he told her she was wrapping a gift for the woman who owned the company she worked for.

He whistled softly as the elevator door reached the ninth floor. Stepping out, he almost knocked over the young man carrying a bottle of wine and two glasses on a silver tray.

The younger man apologized profusely, obviously rattled by the surprise of meeting someone at such a late hour.

"That must be for me," Michael said, as the young man raised his hand to knock on Vanessa's door. The valet gave him a puzzled look, until he realized Michael was opening the door with the electronic hotel key. Michael tipped him before entering the quiet room. He placed the gift on the tray before setting the tray on the edge of the bed.

Vanessa silently stepped out of the bathroom, clicking the light off behind her. Michael looked up from removing his shoes, as she glided on the silent carpet to stand in front of him.

He let out a low whistle as his eyes followed the length of the goddess clad in the peach nightie, starting at the delicately painted coral toenails, leading up to the lacy hem that flowed over her slim ankles. The curve of her hips pulled the silky fabric across the slightly rounded tummy, and again across the small but firm breasts. He swallowed as his eyes focused on the shoulders, glowing a golden colour, bare except for the thin straps and blonde strands that fell across her collar bones. His approving look was all she needed to encourage her to touch him, her fingers unbuttoning for the second time the front of his shirt.

He moaned as she pushed him back with a forceful shove onto the bed. He barely noticed his belt being undone as her hot fingers ran across his sensitive belly.

She shivered as he ran his hands over her back and down the length of her gown, pulling her closer to him, allowing her to feel his hardness as she pressed against him.

He rolled her off him, not ready to be seduced by her, although the thought was not far from being reality. He wanted to give her his gift and move the wine and glasses to a safer place than the bed before they knocked the tray onto the luxuriously carpeted floor.

He sat up, removing the tray to a safer spot on the table then eased himself against the pillows he had propped against the headboard.

Vanessa, confused by his pulling away from her a second time, stared at him with hurt eyes. She was ready for him, wanted him, and she thought he wanted her too. She must be more out of touch as to how to handle a man than she thought she was, she thought with dismay.

"This is for my music box lady," he said, handing a surprised Vanessa a tiny gold box. He watched anxiously as she directed her attention to unwrapping the unexpected present.

"Oh, Michael. It's beautiful." She wrapped an arm around his neck, still clutching the delicately carved music box to her chest. "You know, this is the first music box I have ever owned." The tears trickled down her flushed cheeks. She wiped at them unsuccessfully, as he pulled her closer to him aware of the wet tears cooling his hot skin.

"It won't be the last one, either," he said, smoothing the blonde bangs out of her eyes. She smiled up at him as she shifted to a sitting position on the bed beside him. She lifted the tiny gold-etched lid to listen to the familiar tune once more.

Jumping off the bed suddenly Vanessa raced to the bathroom, setting the music box on the sink counter. A puzzled Michael appeared in the doorway right behind her, a worried expression crossing his handsome face.

She turned to find him blocking the doorway as the soft smack of her gown hit his bare chest. "Oh," she said suddenly realizing what she had done. "Sorry to run out on you like that," she said, a nervous giggle escaping her lips. "I left the tub running. I don't think the management would appreciate the floor flooding over."

"Don't ever run away from me again," he said, half serious, half teasing. His hands gripped her upper arms firmly, forcing her back toward the cool porcelain of the tub. A playful smile flickered on his lips a second before he let her go. A shocked scream escaped from her only to be muffled as she went under, splashing the walls and floor. She came up sputtering, her hair covering her flashing green eyes, as she brushed the soaked strands over her forehead.

"What did you do that for?" she exclaimed, unable to control her laughter when she realized he was laughing at her. She must look a sight, she thought, grabbing a glimpse in the steamy mirror behind him.

He stepped forward, touching her gown where it clung to her breast. The feel of his caress sent shock waves of heat coursing through her body. She stepped out of the tub which wasn't easy with the long gown clinging tightly around her ankles. She would have fallen if it wasn't for his quick reflexes, catching her as she stumbled on the last step.

His deep, throaty laugh echoed in the small room. Her wet body pressed against his, responding instantly to the fluid movement of his hands as they ran up and down her bare, wet back.

She closed her eyes as he continued his gentle massage. His lips found the neat hollows in her neck as he gently kissed her. She moaned in response, running her soft hands across his broad shoulders, feeling the strength and gentleness together at once. Her fingers ran down the length of his spine, making him pull her tightly against him. She could feel his male hardness return. Her eager fingers sought the belt buckle that pressed into her ribcage, making him pull away for the little time it took her to unbuckle it.

The sound of the zipper was followed almost immediately by the thump of the weight of his pants filled with keys and wallet as it hit the floor. She gasped, seeing him in all his male splendor for the first time in the light, as he bent to slip the socks off before lifting her effortlessly off her feet and stepping into the warmth of the waiting tub.

"Let me look at you," he said forcing her to stand up while he pulled the nightie over her head. His appreciative smile turned to an expression of longing in his steel gray eyes. "God, I've missed you."

"I know," she replied, reaching to touch his hair, pushing the few stray strands behind his ear. The heat of the tub rose to cover their naked bodies as he reached a muscular forearm around her slim waist, pulling her tightly against the steaming heat of his body as he slid down the sloped side. He turned her around in one fluid movement, so her back filled the curve of his chest and stomach as the rolling waves massaged their slick bodies.

She relaxed as he gently massaged her whole body, starting at the temples. His expert manipulation of his hands on the sensitive areas of her body made her writhe in anticipation, urging him to take her, to make her his once more. He turned her around to rub her long legs as she leaned back against the opposite wall of the huge tub.

He slid his body into the center of the bathtub, pulling her legs over his muscular hips, bringing her closer to him. She gently stroked his neck as his one hand cupped her behind while the other found a ledge to brace himself as he lifted her out, clinging to him wrapping her legs tighter against him behind his back.

Michael gently nibbled at her breast as it poked in front of his mouth. She writhed in pleasure, hardly aware he was moving them into the awaiting bedroom. In one easy movement, he pulled the crisp sheet back and sat down. His free hand searched the floor for the overnight bag he had dropped earlier. He continued his caresses of her neck and shoulders as she did her part in almost driving him crazy with her tongue which explored his neck and ear as he tore the small package he had brought in anticipation of this moment.

He slid Vanessa's moist bottom to rest on his knees while he guided her hand to help him before lifting her gently on top of him. Her pulsing need met his as he filled her, going slowly at first, the rhythm keeping pace with their increasing heartbeats. She felt his body tense in response to hers, pleasure swept over them in uncontrollable waves until she finally slumped against his gleaming chest, a satisfied smile crossing her pretty mouth. They lay for a long time in each other's arms before he pulled the covers over her sleeping body.

"Do you always wake your women with the smell of fresh coffee?" she asked, yawning loudly.

Michael laughed. "For one thing, I don't have any women to wake with the smell of fresh coffee, except you. And it's just a habit of mine. I need my coffee first thing, sort of a jump-start for me."

"Anyone would need a jump-start after a night like last night," she said, smiling wickedly as he handed her the coffee cup while she struggled to cover her bare chest with the few covers that remained on the bed.

It was his turn to smile. "I think I need more than coffee this morning," he said, leaning over to plant a kiss on her tangled mass of hair. "How about breakfast before you have to return home?"

The thought of having to leave him stabbed at her heart. It was time to come back to reality, she realized, setting the cup on the night table. She noticed that he had already packed and was dressed. He must have showered as she slept, and she hadn't noticed. It was a comfortable feeling having him around, she thought, sadly. She watched as he gathered up the remaining towels and wiped the bathroom mirror. He threw her one of the fluffy towels from the bathroom, as she glanced around the room, looking for something to wrap around herself.

"Thanks," she yelled, over the roar of the water filling the sink as he washed his hands.

"I'll meet you in the restaurant," he said, pulling the navy jacket on, accenting his broad shoulders once again.

She was thankful for the privacy, but missed the closeness of the night before. Why did he keep distancing himself from her? If he wanted her to live with him so badly, why did he act as if they were just having an affair? That is what it is, after all. She had thought that after her trip to Blue River and the thought that it could be true, that he really didn't want her around, saddened her.

The hot shower felt good against her shoulders. She hesitated to use the soap provided by the hotel, knowing it

would remove the sultry scent of him that lingered on her trim
body, but she hadn't packed any soap of her own.

She quickly dried off, ruffling the towel through her thick
hair before dabbing the moisture off her legs and torso. She
wrapped her body with the thick towel before she reached for
the make up bag that contained her comb and other accessories
she needed to make herself presentable.

In less than fifteen minutes she was packed and ready to
go. Noticing that he had taken his belongings with him, she
decided to take hers with her. He had offered her a ride to the
airport, and she decided to take him up on it. She wasn't ready
to say goodbye just yet. She knew she had to, at least for a little
while. In three more weeks he would want her answer. Darn
him, why didn't he propose properly to her before presenting
her with the charming music box, she thought, fighting to
control the tears that welled up. Why couldn't she have fought
the urge and not made love with him last night? Maybe he
wouldn't ask her, knowing how easy it was for her to give in,
he didn't have to marry her to have her.

She was in a dark mood as she entered the bright restaurant. She stood in the doorway for a few seconds before
spotting his big frame in the corner booth. He was looking out
at the traffic whipping past. Vancouver was certainly faster
paced than her own city of Prince George. She knew she
would never want to live here, although it had always proved
full of excitement whenever she ventured through. She watched
him watch the traffic for a few seconds longer, trying to
summon up a bright smile, although what she felt was a deep
sense of loss. It was her decision to keep on with her business,
and she made it quite clear to him. She only hoped she was
making the right decision.

"Hi," she said, sliding across the burgundy leather seat,
opposite him. He had only a coffee cup in front of him, half
full. At least he had waited to eat with her, she thought. Maybe
he just felt she needed her privacy, and hadn't actually meant
to make her feel as if he didn't want to be around her.

"Vanessa," he started, reaching for her hand as she set her

small purse on the windowsill. "I need to know if…"

"Wait. It was I who seduced you this time, Michael, and I'm sorry. I've already told you I won't live with you unless it comes with a marriage certificate, but I also need my work. It fills a void in my life that was there even when I was married. I wish I could make you understand." Vanessa sighed, and cast a glance out the window, unable to meet Michael's sad gray eyes.

"Vanessa, I'm old-fashioned, and jealous of your success. I don't begrudge you any of it," he added quickly when she turned her gaze back to him. "It's just an insecurity I have about the woman I love needing more than what I can offer her that scares me."

"I can't give up the business," she whispered, wondering why she felt so desperately that she would lose what was more valuable in the end.

"And I can't compete with it," he said, quietly. "I'm sorry, Vanessa." Michael's slumped shoulders portrayed his feelings of defeat loudly.

Vanessa watched him in silence as the waitress refilled their coffees.

"Michael, I know it is hard for you to understand my point of view, knowing how much it must have hurt to go through a divorce. Believe me, I wouldn't marry anyone if I thought that is how it would end up. I love you," she admitted, "even if you can't see that. I need to hear the same from you." She stared at his gray eyes, nervously waiting for his response.

"I love you, too, Vanessa." His voice broke, unable to keep the shaking words from falling from trembling lips. "I do love you. I thought you knew that."

Her green eyes softened, moistened by the same tears that threatened only a few minutes ago. "I still need to work at my business," she said softly, barely a whisper.

"I know." His tough features softened for an instant. He glanced out the window, trying to hide the sadness that was evident in his eyes. He knew how important her work was to her, and if there was any way he could think of that would allow her to continue her business and live on the ranch he wished it would come to him.

She sat quietly, realizing this was not the place she would expect a proposal, and she didn't want to encourage it right at the moment. They each had their busy lives to contend with.

"I'm on holiday now for the next two weeks," he said, changing the subject. "Care to spend a few days on the ranch again?" he asked, hopefully.

"Do you ever give up?" she asked, laughing nervously. It was a strange, unfamiliar sound that came from her throat. If he was anything, he was persistent. She liked that quality in him.

"Not when I know what I want," he said, making her blush at the hot look he cast her.

"I'll see how things are going at home. I'll call you, okay?"

"I guess that's all I can hope for at the moment," he said. The waitress arrived to take their orders, ending the conversation for the moment.

They chatted about the race track and arena he had taken her to the day before. She was impressed with his knowledge of thoroughbred horses. She told him how she used to ride every weekend when she was in university, before she met Mark and got married. She had loved to get out into the country and feel the strength of a horse as it galloped beneath her. She was an expert rider, as he had already witnessed.

"Then you must come for another visit, because Rusty doesn't get much exercise anymore. Old Danny Boy is having a hard time keeping up to her, I'm afraid."

"I don't think old Danny Boy has any trouble at all," she said, remembering the quick ride back to the stable when the storm broke, both of them on the big stallion's back. She sensed that he was through pressuring her into coming as he shifted against the back of the leather seat. She followed his gaze out the restaurant window, feeling a sadness overwhelm her as she thought about leaving him to head home.

"I would love to come down again, but you have to change your tune if you think I am coming down just to make love to you. This time, it would be to ride, and enjoy a refreshing holiday—that is, if I did come," she added. Her green eyes glinted in the sunlight that filtered through the glass. A sunny ray cast a warm glow over her golden tresses.

She was ravenous, she suddenly realized as the smell of bacon reminded her of the first morning on the ranch.

The flight was the same quick fifty-five minutes once they left Vancouver International Airport, heading north through the cloudless sky. Vanessa spent the time gazing out the window, enjoying the expansive view of mostly uninhabited British Columbia countryside. The mountain tops were still peaked with snow and green-ice glaciers, even though it was almost June.

It was just after ten the next morning when she arrived at the office.

"Well?" Janice asked, a playful smile crossing her lips.

"Well?" echoed Vanessa, laughing at her obviously satisfied friend. "How was the rest of your weekend?" she inquired, plopping herself on the corner of Janice's desk.

"Wonderful. We went gallivanting around downtown and then we had a lovely dinner last night at the Delta Hotel." Vanessa watched her friend's eyes as they stared dreamily off into space. Yes, she's in love, all right, Vanessa mused.

"I'm going to be in my office for the next couple of hours," Vanessa said. "Screen my calls for me, please. Take messages and I'll get back to them after lunch."

"Sure. No problem."

Vanessa walked slowly down the hallway, noticing the pictures of the ballerinas as if for the first time. She stopped to look at the tiny box pictured on the poster at the end of the hall. She stepped closer, not believing her eyes. It was the exact music box Michael had bought for her. He must have remembered it and bought it in one of her stores in Vancouver. No, she thought, that is too unlikely. It must be a fluke.

She closed the door slowly behind her. The smooth pane of glass with her name etched in gold felt cool to the touch. She ran her fingers across her name, wondering if she really wanted to keep the business. She had put in four tough years learning it, making it profitable, but maybe Michael was right; it was time to sell it. The thought of giving it up made her shiver involuntarily at the idea of losing her identity with it.

After setting her purse on the broad desk top, she walked around it to open the curtains. The view from the second floor window was starting to become overgrown with new buildings. She used to enjoy visiting Mark, and looking out over the Nechako River, but the development around her was beginning to eat up the lush greenery.

She sighed as she strolled over to the bookcase filled with many of the favorite novels she used to read while waiting for Mark to finish in a meeting. She never did take any of the books home, knowing that they were read and enjoyed in the presence of this room, with its comfortable love seat, and quietly understated elegance. She was also reluctant to let the memory of Mark's existence escape from the very room he was so proud to have created.

The longer she dwelled on the thought of selling the business, the more anxious she got. If she did sell, and married Michael, could she be happy being only his wife, and having to go through the loneliness again whenever he went out of town? She thought not. It was tough enough the first time. She realized she wasn't prepared to do it again. Still, she found her heart was not in the running of the business like it was before she met him. She cursed him softly under her breath.

She leafed through the morning mail, then went to the computer set up in the far corner on a discreet desk. She accessed the files she needed and reviewed the weekend's business from all her stores. Victoria had done exceptionally well, she noted, even though most of Jason's weekend had been tied up in meeting with her. She was suitably impressed with his enthusiasm and knowledge of the business. She would think about promoting him if she could come up with a suitably challenging position for the favorite young manager.

The week passed quickly for Vanessa, making her feel

even more restless about her indecision about the company. She called Jason to talk about the business, and found herself inviting him to Prince George for the weekend to have a look around at the head office. He was thrilled and she was glad of his reaction. He certainly had a few good ideas she was thinking of implementing, and he was all for the incentive program. He had read extensively on the subject as well, and he surprised her with some facts she had overlooked.

Vanessa gave Janice the pleasure of picking Jason up at the airport, dropping him off at his hotel, before returning to work late Friday afternoon.

"Is he all settled?" Vanessa asked Janice. Janice's face glowed from seeing him again, Vanessa noted, as Janice entered the office.

"Yes, I told him you would be over as soon as the store closed." Vanessa nodded, smiling at her friend. Janice had made the suggestion that she make an offer to Jason to accept the position of general manager, but for some reason Vanessa felt he would do whatever he felt was best for him, no matter what she offered.

"Do you really think he will accept the position?" Janice had trouble hiding the excitement in her voice.

"I can't see why not. There aren't many men his age that get offered the position of GM in a company this size." She hoped he would seriously consider her offer.

The last few days she had been figuring out what she wanted to do with the rest of her life, and she didn't picture herself sitting behind the great oak desk. The thought of living with Michael, provided he proposed marriage to her, kept cropping up in her brain whenever she wasn't concentrating on anything in particular, which happened for longer periods, since her last encounter with him.

Jason was waiting in the lobby when Vanessa walked in. His navy suit and blue tie suddenly made her think it was Michael sitting there in the comfort of the lobby. She took a deep breath, trying to compose herself, before striding over to him. After exchanging pleasantries, Vanessa led the way to the dining lounge where she had reserved a quiet table in the corner.

"You look distracted," she said after taking a quick sip of the delicate wine.

"Oh, it's nothing. I just thought, well, Janice would be joining us." His bright blue eyes sparkled with adoration for the woman who had entered his life in the short span of a week.

"Actually, she decided to opt out, allowing me to talk to you with no distraction. She is coming over here later to join us."

His face brightened, then reddened. "Please don't think I just came up here to see her," he said, hastily. "The position you offered was rather intriguing."

"Don't worry, I don't." She gave him an endearing look before getting down to business. "If you are going to be my general manager, I need you here in Prince George to run the head office, and help with the relocation." His surprised expression was replaced with a smile as he realized she was talking about his suggestion of moving the head office to Victoria. "It's time I took a step down from doing most of the work around here. I think you're the one who can handle it." She held her breath, watching his reaction.

Jason's blue eyes widened. "You're seriously thinking of handing over the reins."

"Very," she said, suddenly realizing that his choice of words pulled her heartstrings tighter for a split second. She would love to trade in her reins for some of Michael's if she could. It was time.

Her cool green eyes assessed the young man in front of her. He was a few years younger than she, but had the business background and education she had learned the hard way. She hadn't made a mistake in choosing him. "I'll need your answer soon," she said.

"Does that mean you're going ahead with the relocation?"

Vanessa nodded. "I think so, but I'll sleep on it tonight. You'll have my answer in the morning." He rose quickly as Janice approached. Vanessa smiled, shook his hand, and reached for the check. "My treat," he said, beating her to it. She liked him.

The next day Vanessa was greeted by a smiling Jason waiting outside the store doors. "I decided to accept your offer," he said, breathless, as if he had run all the way from the hotel. By the looks of his hair he had, she thought, amused and pleased at having someone so excited working for her.

"Come inside. I'll start some coffee."

"No need to," Janice said, walking rapidly up behind them. "Here you go. Black, you said, didn't you, Jason?" she asked, handing him the steaming cup.

"Right," he said, wrapping an arm around her shoulder as they stepped inside.

Vanessa glanced at the two of them, acutely aware of her longing to have Michael near her, touching her. She was going to take him up on his invitation, planning to call as soon as she was finished ironing out the details of Jason's new position.

The morning dragged as Vanessa went over every aspect of the business Jason was not familiar with, but she was impressed and pleased by how quickly he caught on. Janice left them alone, undisturbed for the most part, intruding only to bring a few donuts and fresh pot of coffee.

"I'm thinking of asking Janice to marry me," Jason blurted out as Vanessa stopped to pour another cup of steaming coffee. Her hand shook, almost dropping the cup onto the smooth carpet.

"What?" she gasped, shock filling her eyes.

Jason flushed. "I love her, and I want her to be with me. You won't be needing her now that you are relinquishing so many of your duties to me. I could keep her working for me as long as she likes, in Victoria."

"Have you discussed this with Janice?"

"Yes, actually. This morning over breakfast." His eyes sparkled with adoration as he explained his plan. Janice could stay here as long as Vanessa needed her, until the office was relocated. Then they would get married in Victoria. "She loves it there," he added, at last.

"I know," Vanessa said, wistfully. "I'm happy for you both." She tried to sound joyful, but it came out forced. How could Janice know he was the one for her, when they only met last week? She was still struggling with her passion for Michael, envious of Janice's obvious certainty of what was right for her. She wished she had the same conviction about life that her friend, Janice, did.

Appearing in the doorway, Janice suggested that they both take a break for lunch. Vanessa, happy to have an excuse to be alone, suggested they take the rest of the afternoon off together, and congratulated them both again. Janice beamed.

Vanessa closed the door behind them, sighing deeply as she crumpled into the softness of the love seat. She rubbed the back of her neck, trying to take the kinks out that had worked their way into her shoulders too. If only Michael were here, she thought, she would have him massage the knots out with his expert fingers.

She closed her eyes. Michael. If only he were here. But he had said she was invited down to the ranch again if she wanted to visit. Boy, did she want to visit. Almost a week had passed since their night in Vancouver, which didn't last nearly long enough, she thought, her body stirring warmly at the memory. She would have to call him. He wasn't about to make the first move and she knew it.

She pushed herself up off the love seat, and reached for the phone that sat at the corner of her desk. She dialed the number that was still tucked in the corner of the blotter. It rang seven, eight, nine times. Damn. Where was he when she needed him?

Vanessa strolled through the hallways and back rooms of the offices, speaking briefly to the employees as she came upon them. Some stopped to thank her for setting up the incentive program, others just smiled. Vanessa suddenly felt more lonely than she could ever remember in her life. Maybe just the fact that Janice seemed to have found someone, and without much effort, was what seemed to make her loneliness all the more depressing.

Why was it so difficult for her to come to terms with her

relationship with Michael? Was he really that adamant about her living with him, not getting married, in case she wanted out of the marriage? Why couldn't he take a chance on love the second time? After all, wasn't that what she was doing? Wasn't she? She returned to the quiet solitude of her office, gathered her things, and locked up behind her. This trip she was determined to find the answers.

Nine

The phone stopped ringing the moment he reached it. Michael took a deep breath, and slammed the receiver down. Damn. Why was he feeling so frustrated lately? Les was back and helping out. It should be a pleasant two week vacation on the ranch with no booking of seminars or hotel arrangements to be made.

He had put his business phone on an answering machine, but it was his personal line that was ringing. He rarely gave out that number. He suddenly thought of Vanessa, the last person he had given it to. Was that her on the phone? Had she changed her mind about spending time on the ranch? With him?

Why wouldn't she come visit? The invitation had been open enough. He stomped out of the kitchen, heading to his bedroom to change out of his work clothes. He didn't really feel like eating, but forced himself to make a half-decent meal before retiring in front of the television. After a half hour of flicking the channels back and forth, he clicked it off. Even that didn't help him take his mind off her.

Nothing worked. The thought of her willing body, soft and warm against his, evoked the desire he had been trying to quell ever since he dropped her off at the airport earlier this week. She had been eager to return to work, he thought. There was no way he could tie her down to marrying him and staying on the ranch. Just hearing her talk about her business, he could feel the excitement she found in running it. He knew the feeling. Being your own boss, doing your own thing sure had its benefits.

He finally had to take a cold shower before heading for bed. Maybe he was wrong about marriage. Maybe it would work out for them. After all, she had said she wouldn't live with him, not that she wouldn't marry him. But was he ready? What if it didn't work out? What if she did sell the business? What would she do on a ranch in Blue River?

Vanessa tried his number once more before retiring. She let it ring six times, holding her breath, waiting for his deep voice to answer. Still, there was none. She felt miserable as she changed into her nightie while Charlie pushed his way into the stillness of her bedroom.

"Will I have to sleep with a cat forever?" she asked the purring furball, who obviously would not mind it one bit if things remained the same. Reaching for her book that she left on the night table, she thought how lonely it would be to spend the rest of her life sleeping single.

Saturday morning came early, too early for Vanessa. The covers on her bed had been pulled out of their neatly tucked corners, evidence of her sleepless night. As usual, Michael had occupied her mind for most of the waking moments. She had finally fallen asleep as the light of dawn poked its sharp fingers through the crack in the closed curtains.

It was just after nine when the phone rang. Deep in thought, she jumped at the intrusion, almost dropping the piece of bread dripping egg for French toast onto the cream linoleum floor.

"Hi! How are you?" the tantalizing voice murmured in her ear.

"Michael. Where are you?" she asked, surprised to hear from him. "I tried calling…"

"I'm in Prince George, at the hotel. I need to see you," he said, an unfamiliar urgency evident in his voice.

Vanessa's eyes widened. She wasn't even dressed. Hastily she turned off the grill and poured the batter down the sink as she held the phone tucked between her shoulder and ear. Her stomach started to flip-flop so suddenly she didn't think she could eat anything now.

"Why, what's up?" She tried to keep the alarm out of her voice.

"Nothing, I just wanted to see you. Can you meet me, or can I stop by your place?"

"Well, I…sure." She quickly gave directions, knowing he had about fifteen minutes driving to reach the house. That barely gave her enough time to make herself presentable and tidy up a bit. The housework had been taking the brunt of her lack of desire to do anything outside of the business for the past couple of weeks.

She made fast work of getting dressed, scrubbing her face vigorously to put some colour back into it. She applied mascara and a little blush. That would have to do, she thought, as she put the things back into their proper places before heading back into the kitchen to start a fresh pot of coffee.

The soft rapping on the front door set her heart to racing, her palms becoming moist instantly. She rubbed them along the sides of her jeans before opening the door with trembling hands.

He stood there, waiting for her to invite him in. He seemed taller, until she remembered she was standing in bare feet. His soft gray eyes dispelled the last of the nervousness she felt.

"It's good to see you. Come in. I've been thinking about you." She led him by the hand, closing the heavy wooden door behind them.

Michael surveyed the interior of the well-kept little house. It was certainly cozy, not the type of place he suspected she might want to give up if he asked her to marry him, he thought, with confidence waning. He swallowed before he spoke.

"There is a lot we have to talk about, but right now," he said, pulling her to an abrupt halt as they stepped into the brightly lit kitchen, "I just want to look at you." He gazed at her warm eyes, peachy skin glowing in the pleasure of seeing him again.

"Oh, Vanessa, I missed you so much," he said. His warm breath caressed her exposed ear. She felt the fire course through her as if his breath in her ear was the oxygen she needed to rekindle the spark that continued to glow inside her. Instantly she was in his arms, pressing her cheek to the strong, beating chest, clad in a white cotton shirt, tucked neatly into the skin tight jeans that looked so good on him.

Her hair had been hastily tied back into a pony tail at the nape of her neck, but it didn't last long when he ran his fingers around the back of her head, pressing his lips to her warm, wet ones, eager to taste the fruit of his long wait. He slid the thick covered-elastic band down the length of her short pony tail, releasing the sweet-smelling golden tresses he had longed to touch all week.

"Mmm, I missed you, too," she murmured, feeling the tingling sensation as he wrapped her in his strong embrace, acutely aware of the tantalizing scent of his cologne. He squeezed her tightly before releasing her. She stepped back, allowing herself the luxury of basking in his avid approval of her.

Turning to the counter that held the coffee pot, she tried to focus on something other than his overwhelming sexuality. It was difficult, she admitted to herself. Less than half an hour ago she was trying to put him out of her mind, unable to contact him the night before. Suddenly he was there, standing in her kitchen, his tall frame filling the room with his masculinity.

She tried to remember the last time a man was in her kitchen, and it surprised her to have to struggle to grasp an image of Mark being there, even though it was only four years ago. She smiled, feeling a kind of peace overcome her. The comfortable feeling of being with Michael no longer brought the uneasy feeling she used to have whenever she was around another man other than Mark.

She placed two steaming cups of black coffee on the counter that separated the kitchen from the dining room. His tanned hand covered hers for an instant, sending shockwaves of desire coursing through her body. She leaned over the counter, watching him as he settled on the bar stool that served as her seat most mornings when she read the news while having her breakfast.

"Are you hungry?" she asked, suddenly realizing she hadn't eaten yet.

"Only for you," he replied, a crooked grin played under his mustache. Vanessa blushed. A soft laugh escaped her parted lips.

He had such an exciting effect on her, she knew, wanting him to pursue the topic more. But she realized they had to come to an agreement with their relationship before things became too complicated.

"Michael, I…I tried to call you last night. I was going to take you up on your offer to visit your ranch this week." She stopped, sipping her coffee while watching his with green eyes peeking through the bangs that clouded her vision.

Michael's heart thumped, picking up the pace. Visit his ranch, he noted. She hadn't said visit him. His face softened, wondering if she had an answer to his suggestion of living with him, but he was afraid to ask. What if she said no? Could he handle losing her? He frowned as he continued his silent assessment.

"You still can if you want to," he said. He reached into his back pocket and produced two packages that resembled airline tickets and plopped them on the counter in front of her.

"But I thought you might like to have a more exciting vacation than that."

Vanessa gasped as she opened the top one. In it was the itinerary for a week in Vancouver, hotels booked, reservations made by the travel agent.

"Oh, Michael, you shouldn't have done this. I can pay for my own vacation, if I wanted to go anywhere."

"I know, but I wanted you to spend a week with me in Vancouver. We could take a ferry to Victoria, drive up to Nanaimo and take the ferry to the Sunshine Coast. I've booked a hotel in Sechelt already. I just have to call to confirm it. What do you say?" His excitement and pleasure filled the cozy kitchen.

"It sounds great." Vanessa smiled, wondering when she was going to get up the courage to tell him she needed him to make a commitment. If only a marriage proposal came with the vacation, she could consider the trip their honeymoon. Deciding to take the plunge and get it over with, she cleared her throat.

"Michael, I've been thinking, and I've decided I want to sell the business."

"What? I thought you loved it," he said, placing his cup down heavily onto the counter, sloshing a bit out of it. Vanessa quickly grabbed a paper towel and soaked it up, thankful for the moment's distraction to collect her thoughts.

"I do, but I've found the perfect person to be my general manager." She went on to explain the week's events to a quietly amused Michael.

"That sounds like a great idea," he said, when she explained she was going to move the head office to Victoria. Maybe there was hope that she would move in with him.

"But he will still report to me on a daily basis until I find a suitable buyer. I want it to be someone who will care as much for my people and the business as I do."

He nodded. His heart plummeted. That meant that she could be tied down for quite some time. He did admire her dedication though.

"What will you do when it sells?" he asked, staring directly at her. She couldn't avoid his probing eyes, but was afraid to look directly at him. She busied herself pouring more coffee, her head bent so that the mass of waves covered her softened features.

When she was growing up, Vanessa had always dreamed of raising horses, but it had never been feasible in her life before. Now she had toyed with the idea of raising horses herself, but not in Prince George. However, she was not about to open that subject with him. He would most certainly want her to start that on his ranch, live with him and raise them there. She felt a twinge of guilt in keeping the idea to herself, but it wasn't fully developed yet, and she was just starting to think about it. It was a dream she'd had before she married, but she never had the chance to pursue it. Selling the business would give her the capital she needed to buy some property to start out. But first she had to sell it.

Changing the subject, she picked up the ticket envelopes again and leafed inside. The memory of their night in the city warmed her again. It was tempting to just fall into his strong arms and say yes to whatever he wanted. But she struggled to keep her head clear of the emotions that flooded every inch of her body while he was in the vicinity.

"My month isn't up yet, and you want me to take a trip with you, all expenses paid, right?" She tapped the tickets onto the counter, fidgeting with the edges.

"You know I can't wait forever, but I did give you a month. I never said I wouldn't bug you about it. Vanessa," he said, walking around to her side of the counter, "I need you with me, one way or another."

"You sure have a way with words," she said, holding back the urge to kiss his irresistible lips. Instead she ran her fingers along his clean-shaven chin, lingering momentarily, before touching his lips with her finger.

Michael reached her hand, and held her, nibbling on the fingertips that were teasing him beyond control. He had to have her, needed her to be his.

"Are you coming with me?" he asked, glancing at the ticket she held in her other hand.

"Yes," she said, sighing in surrender. "How can I pass up such an offer?" she teased. "I guess I can make arrangements for Janice to cover in my absence. I'll have to pack quickly if we are going to make the flight out this afternoon."

He nodded, kissing her quickly on the forehead. "You go pack and call Janice. I'll clean up in here," he said, releasing his grip on her. He watched, smiling in satisfaction, as she strolled out of the room. Well, he had less than a week to convince her that she should live with him. Hearing that she wanted to sell the business had been a shock to him, especially after hearing her adamantly defend her position on keeping the company the last time he saw her. There was hope yet, he thought, smiling to himself as he placed the cups in the sink and ran the water.

She could hardly believe she was going with him. There was no denying she wanted to be with him, above all else, and the fact that she was eagerly packing proved it. But he still hadn't mentioned marriage. Maybe they would get the chance to discuss it later this week, she thought, as she stuffed as many clean clothes as she could into her suitcase.

She called Janice, giving her a brief explanation of what had to be done at work, and instructions on when to feed Charlie and where to find the spare key.

The Prince George Airport was not very busy when they checked in. There was just the one boarding room with two exits and they placed bets as to which exit they would be using.

They arrived at Vancouver International Airport right on schedule. Vanessa linked her arm through Michael's as they picked up the pace walking through the long corridor and down the escalator to eventually arrive at the baggage area. It was raining lightly outside, but they didn't mind. His car was parked close to the exit. They strolled slowly carrying their luggage and enjoying each other's company.

Michael stopped to check into the hotel first, before taking

Vanessa for an unscheduled flight. After carrying their bags into the room, he smiled at her, his eyes twinkling mischievously as he opened his suitcase to find a change of clothes.

"Better put on a sweater, and change into your jeans. It may get a little chilly."

"What's wrong with what I have on?" she asked, looking down at the neat slacks and blouse, topped with a favorite mandarin style jacket.

"I just think you'd be more comfortable in jeans, where we're going." A slow smile escaped his lips, intent on not giving her anymore hints.

Vanessa tried, but couldn't drag any more information out of him. His secrecy peaked her curiosity and the only way she was going to discover what he was up to was to do as he asked. She resigned herself to digging through her suitcase, pulling out a pressed pair of denims and a cozy multi-coloured sweater.

"Just give me a hint," she said, pulling the sweater over her head, shaking the loose tresses into a fluffy fullness.

"It's a surprise," he said, watching her wiggle into the tight fitting jeans she brought. It was difficult to suppress the urge to tear them off her, but Michael stood patiently waiting for her before easing her out the hotel room door.

Vanessa's stomach hatched butterflies as she realized he was heading to Langley Airport where she could see several hot air balloons at different stages of flight. She glanced at him sideways, wondering if that was where he intended to take her. She didn't have to wait long to find out.

"Here we are," he said, a pleased sound reflecting in his voice.

"You've got to be kidding! You're not getting me up in one of those," indicating one of the few hot air balloons that were looming overhead. Vanessa crossed her arms and sat rigidly in her seat. Michael had to open her door and haul her out, fighting her all the way.

"Come on, Vanessa. It'll be an adventure. You said yourself that your sister is always after you to take a chance. Now's your chance."

She stared at him in disbelief, knowing he was serious and wouldn't let up.

"Okay, okay, but if I get sick…"

"You won't. Trust me." He guided her to the hot air balloon that he had rented. The weather was perfect for ballooning, and he was glad he had booked a balloon earlier. The flights were always dependent upon the weather. The winds couldn't be blowing south, as they could be flown across the Canada-US border, which would cause a lot of problems.

He helped her in. She clung to the side of the huge basket, feeling not too well when he rocked the basket slightly as he hopped in. Then quickly he prepared for take-off.

"You've done this before?" she asked in amazement, turning to watch him as he switched on the fan that blew the hot air into the balloon, forcing them to lift gently off the ground.

"I used to come out here when I was in university. It wasn't as popular as it is now, but I got my pilot's license then and I usually manage a few flights every year."

Vanessa groaned. "I can't believe we're doing this."

"Don't worry. I know what I'm doing." His reassuring words soothed her, but only somewhat. She still had a hold of the side with both hands. They were rising higher and higher, faster and faster.

Michael gently touched her shoulder, motioning for her to look in the direction he was pointing. The whole of Vancouver could be seen from their vantage point, more than the glimpse they had while in the airplane. He turned the motor off and let them glide through the air. A gentle breeze blew through the opening below the balloon, making it harder to be heard.

Vanessa had to raise her voice. "Okay, I've had enough. How do you get this thing down?"

"Just a minute." He turned to the wicker basket that was stored inside before they took off. Opening it up, he retrieved a bottle of champagne and two crystal glasses that were held in place by an elastic clip to the side of the basket.

"What's that for?" she asked, eyes wide in amazement. Michael was certainly into surprises, she thought. First the balloon ride, now champagne. Just what she needed, to get drunk in the middle of the open sky. She extended a shaking hand to accept the offered glass, still holding tightly in the softly swaying basket.

"It's for a toast."

"What are we celebrating?"

"You being here, with me." His gray eyes penetrated hers as she looked up into his handsome face. His serious expression made her smile.

"What are you smiling about?"

"You being here, with me." She echoed his phrase, reaching for his glass as he tried to pop the cork.

"Sounds serious," he said. "Made up your mind yet?" he asked, pouring first hers, then his.

"You take me twelve hundred feet above the ground, ply me with liquor, then ask me if I've made my mind up?" she asked, incredulously. "What if I haven't? Are you going to keep me here until I give you the answer you want?" She felt helpless, yet annoyed with him. He had a lot of nerve taking her up in one of these things, she thought as she tried not to look down.

"That would be nice, but I have other surprises in mind."

She couldn't help but laugh when she saw the mischievous gleam in his eyes. She never could stay angry at him for long, she knew. The wind whistled through the open basket, making her shiver suddenly.

"Chilly? Come here, I'll warm you up," he said, removing the empty glass she held and placing it in the holder in the wicker basket beside his.

She rolled into his strong embrace, reveling in his masculine scent. Having had only one glass of champagne she knew she was still in control of her senses, but something about him was making her crazy, reckless.

Michael's slowly roving hands warmed every inch of her body, whether he touched the spot or not.

Vanessa sighed, leaning back against him, allowing him to nuzzle at her neck. She reached her arms up to run her fingers through his hair, meeting his waiting mouth with her own. His hands sought their way under her sweater, resting just below her breasts. She inhaled quickly as his fingers ran over her bra, making her senses run with the wind.

"Michael, you're not thinking…"

"You're right, I'm not thinking," he said, turning her around to face him as he continued to run his hands along her back, up under her sweater, unhooking her bra in one easy motion.

She felt the pressure of his hands roving over her body, making her hunger to touch his own bare skin. His hands followed the bumps of her spine, running over the seat of her pants and up to the button in front as he gently pushed her midsection away from him.

"Michael, not here," she whispered between breaths, pulling his wrists downward unsuccessfully. He was slowly driving her wild with his expert use of his fingers as they ran the length of her mid-section, now free from the confinements of the zipper. His familiar hands eased into her jeans, slipping under her panties as he gently pushed them over her smooth hips and buttocks.

She raised her hand to his shoulders, running her fingers down his tight biceps, and down to the top of his own jeans, searching to find the button of his pants, fumbling momentarily in her eagerness to unleash his pent-up male desire. Kissing him feverishly, she pushed the trousers to just above his ankles with a free foot, making him shiver visibly before he pulled her closer, parting her legs to position himself to find her hidden treasures.

He braced himself with one arm against the basket to steady himself as his impatient desire to explore her feminine recess beckoned him to squeeze her against him. The warmth of him penetrated her, as she cried out in the open sky. The urgency that took them both, carried her higher than she ever remembered going. Her knees weakened as she felt the peak of her climax as he joined her in soaring ecstasy.

Vanessa leaned against his chest, being held up only by the sheer strength of his arms as she felt him reach over her, steadying them both, as he lowered her spent body to the bottom of the basket after straightening her clothes for her.

"That was lovely," she said, snuggling in closely as she reached over to refill the glasses, handing one to Michael.

"Mmm," he murmured. "Convinced you yet?" he teased.

She poked him in the ribs, making him spill his drink on his pant leg.

"Guess not." He smiled down at her as her glowing face told him what he didn't hear from her lips. He wondered if it was the right moment to spring his next surprise on her. But first he had to maneuver this contraption back to the ground.

Ten

"I didn't know we were coming here," Vanessa said, surprise evident in her voice. Michael glanced at the woman sitting quietly in the passenger seat of his red Camaro. She had been unusually quiet since the ride in the balloon and it bothered him.

"Just wait. I have someone I want you to meet." He pulled to an abrupt stop, jamming the gear shift into park, before swinging his long legs out the door.

She took a deep breath of the smell of horses, manure and hay mixed together, reminding her of her short stay on the ranch. What was she doing with him again? She made it so easy for him. She chastised herself silently the whole way out to the arena for being so quick to take him up on his offer of a getaway together. He'd never have to stop long enough to make a commitment if she continued to jump into his arms every time he turned around.

"Why are we going into the barn?" she asked, picking her way carefully around the droppings that had not yet been cleaned up. If she had known she would be coming here, she would have worn her boots.

"Hey, Mikey," the scratchy old voice called from inside the darkness of the barn. "Over here. You're just in time." Michael guided Vanessa, holding her hand as she followed behind.

"Jake, how's it going?"

The scratchy voice laughed. "Same as usual," he said, rising to greet his guests.

Vanessa watched as the huge frame of a man stood up, but not until he gently placed the head of the tiny colt on the clean pile of hay.

"What happened? Where's the mare?" Michael asked, concern filling his voice. Vanessa watched in silence, awed by the gentleness Jake portrayed toward the nearly helpless animal.

"Had a difficult birth. She'll be okay in a few days, but this little guy needs attention now. Guess I was nominated."

"You always had a soft spot for orphans," Michael said, remembering the days he spent following Jake around when as a young boy his grandfather would allow him to tag along on a horse buying trip.

Vanessa bent down to stroke the colt's sleek neck.

"Wanna feed him?" the old fellow asked, poking the half-emptied bottle into her hand.

"I'd love to." Vanessa took over, unperturbed by the mess she was getting on her form-fitting jeans. "Michael, he's beautiful."

"Do you like him?"

"I think he's precious. So delicate, but yet so strong. I haven't seen a colt this young since I left the farm in Nova Scotia."

"We named him Tea Bag, 'cause of his colourin'." Jake

stepped back, allowing her room to stretch out on the fresh hay that had been laid in the stall earlier that morning.

Michael felt Jake's hand on his arm. He glanced at his friend, noticing the worried looked etched on his weary face.

"Can I talk to ya for a minute?" Jake asked, glancing nervously at the woman and colt who sat contentedly together. Vanessa and Michael exchanged glances as Jake continued, "Alone."

Vanessa nodded, watching as the two men, approximately the same height and build, walked out of the barn into the misty drizzle. She returned her attention to the sleepy colt who had given up the bottle for a more comfortable position of resting his heavy head in her lap. Vanessa sighed, continuing to stroke the animal's face and neck lovingly, humming quietly to the colt.

"Ya know, I think your pretty lady there likes ol' Tea Bag in there," Jake said once they were out of earshot, tossing his head in the direction they had come.

"Looks that way," Michael said, smiling. He was pleased to find Vanessa so responsive to such a helpless animal. It actually surprised him. After the encounters with his dog, he wasn't too sure how she would handle any animals, except maybe a full grown horse, which she had no trouble handling, he recalled.

"Maybe ya wanna talk to Johnson."

Michael gave him a puzzled look. Johnson was the owner of the stables, a long-time associate of his grandfather's. "Why?"

Jake lowered his voice even though they could not be overheard. "Seems he don't wanna spend the money to raise a new young 'un. There's been five this year, and they're all beauts. Ol' Tea Bag here, he's from good stock, but not great stock, if ya know what I mean." Jake's faded blue eyes pleaded silently with Michael.

Michael glanced over his shoulder to confirm that Vanessa was still unable to hear them. He looked at his friend, noticing the pleading but unspoken words reflected in his eyes.

"Jake, you know I don't have the time to spend with such a young colt." Michael knew Jake was suggesting the colt would be a good buy, because they both knew that the mares at the stable were only bred with the best around, but he wasn't sure now was a good time to raise a new colt. "Even Les is finding it hard to stay on top of everything while I'm on business. I can't add looking after a new colt on him now." Michael shrugged, his shoulders heavy with the knowledge that he was disappointing a dear old friend.

"Just give it some thought. He's only got a week before Johnson starts looking for a buyer. This one's got great potential, I know it." The plea in his faded blue eyes was not lost on his younger friend.

"I'll have to think about it."

"Don't wait too long, a week's all he's got."

"Thanks," Michael mumbled, turning back to get Vanessa, forcing a smile onto his troubled face.

Vanessa returned his smile, detecting a hint of something wrong. "Everything all right?" she asked, gently placing the colt's head onto a soft pile of hay.

"Fine. We better be going now, though, if we're going to get you cleaned up before dinner. Thanks, again, Jake."

"Ya know where to reach me," Jake answered, smiling at his friend, nodding to Vanessa. "Nice seein' you again," he added.

Michael was silent on the way back to the hotel. Vanessa didn't say anything, wondering what was playing on his mind. When they arrived in the room, she could no longer stand it.

"Michael, what did Jake say back there?" she demanded.

He sighed heavily, tossed the keys on the dresser, and grabbed her by the waist to pull her closer. "Nothing for you to worry about," he said, gently kissing the soft bangs that covered her forehead. He was formulating a plan to start a riding stable, in hopes of maybe enticing Vanessa to run it, if he could only be sure she wouldn't think he was buying her a new job. He didn't want to risk upsetting her again about the possibility of selling her business.

His caresses followed the length of her silky neck, as she willingly tossed her head back, enjoying the wonderful sensation of his hot lips as he moved farther down her throat. She moaned softly as his one arm held her to him, while the other undid the few buttons that separated them.

Her hot fingers traveled the length of his straight spine, making his insides quiver as she lightly touched the soft flesh above his waist. She freed his shirt from its tight fit, releasing the pressure on his pants as she undid the buckle and zipper that held his manhood in check.

She slid her arms out of her blouse as he flung it onto the chair beside them. Her bra suffered the same fate, leaving her exposed to his rapturous gaze.

His mouth covered first one nipple, then the other, making her heart pound faster, about to explode in her creamy-skinned chest. She was barely able to stop him long enough to tear his shirt off, making the heat of their bare skin sizzle in the fire of their union. He slipped his hand over her bottom, pulling her jeans and panties off in one quick motion.

Seconds later she was lying on the soft queen-sized bed, enjoying his gentle touch and kisses that flowed over her body like melted honey. She reveled in the sensations that coursed through her as his hands stroked the soft flesh of her inner thighs, working their way up to the moistness that awaited him.

He struggled out of his remaining clothes with her help. The warmth of her skin tantalized his own heated body as he pressed into her softness. He groaned softly as her hot tongue found his ear, her teeth holding his earlobe, making him unable to move away from her hot breath.

"I need you now," she whispered, clutching his firm shoulders as she arched her back in response to his touches.

"I'm not ready, my wallet is in my pants." He gasped as her fingers ran the length of his manhood, nearly driving him crazy with unbridled passion.

"Forget it," she whispered. "It's okay, we already took a chance today," she breathed into his ear, pulling him closer on top of her. The thought of getting pregnant crossed her mind, lingering only long enough for her to realize that having his child would be the ultimate joy. His pulsing heat penetrated her, sending her into spasms of sheer ecstasy, leaving her spent and satisfied.

They awoke in each other's arms a short while later. The cooling breeze from the slightly opened window made him shiver involuntarily as he reached for a sheet to cover them. He kissed her gently on each eyelid, watching them flutter open. The emerald green eyes shone with the most magnificent brightness he could imagine as she smiled up at him. She ran her free hand through his tousled hair.

"Time for dinner, don't you think?" he asked, pulling the sheet off them both. "And you need a shower as badly as I do," he said, laughing. He scooped her naked body into his strong arms, her long legs flailing as she grabbed for his neck.

"Michael, I can walk," she protested, laughing.

"I know, but you feel so good," he said, staring at her pinkish face. She tossed her hair back, gently grazing his strong chin with the soft tresses. "Don't cut your hair," he murmured, setting her down on the cool bathroom counter.

"I can do as I please," she teased.

"As a favor to me, then," he said, staring deeply into her eyes. He then turned his attention to getting the water temperature just right before pulling her into the shower with him, sliding the glass door closed behind her.

"I want you more than you probably realize," he said. The pounding of the water against the wall drowned out his last statement, but he still knew it was true. How was he going to get his green-eyed beauty to believe it? He allowed the pulsing spray to cleanse his body before exchanging places with a half-lathered Vanessa.

"This shower with a friend is being taken a bit too far," she sputtered as the force of the water met with his soapy head. Michael chuckled, reaching for a towel as he stepped out, leaving her to finish her shower in privacy. The fact was, he was getting aroused by her again, and he knew they would not get out of the hotel room all week if he didn't watch himself. He focused on the plans for the week as he dried off quickly, rubbing the rough towel along his muscular legs.

She ran her hands over her wet hair, gently squeezing the last of the water out that she could before stepping out of the shower. She reached for the towel that was stuffed into the little wire rack above the toilet, and yanked it out. She rubbed her face briskly, then wrapped her hair in the towel before grabbing the next one, which was slightly longer than her torso, but not too much.

She walked into the main room. Finding Michael clad only in his white undershorts and socks, she sat down beside him. Only then did she notice the troubled look reappear again on his otherwise handsome face.

"What's the matter?" she asked, gently brushing his forehead with the palm of her hand. He didn't move when she touched him.

"It's nothing." He pushed himself off the corner of the bed, squatting down to find a clean pair of slacks in his suitcase that still laid on the floor. Vanessa admired the lean, muscular back, felt the heat rise in her as her eyes followed the length of his long, tanned legs.

She forced herself to concentrate on getting herself ready or they'd never get out for dinner, she thought, although it wasn't such a bad idea. Something about him was making her care less and less about anything but being with him, in his arms, feeling his heat inside her. She shook her head to clear it. Something was certainly troubling him but she didn't know how to drag it out of him.

"What should I wear?" she asked, a playful smile crossed her pretty face. "Will we be going to a nice restaurant, or a bar and grill?" She tried to remove the heavy feeling that hung in the air between them.

He continued to keep his back to her as he pulled his slacks on. He struggled with the desire to tell her to dress for room service, but thought better of it. If they made love too often without protection, anything could happen. Something could have happened already, he realized. He tried not to think about it, although the fact that she could be carrying his baby was not an upsetting thought.

"Vanessa," he said, turning to face the beautiful green-eyed goddess he had fallen in love with. "I love you."

Vanessa looked up from buttoning her aqua-coloured blouse, surprise evident on her shining face. "Oh, Michael," she said, "you have the weirdest timing." His questioning look prompted her to continue. "I was just thinking that you were feeling…" She fumbled for the right words. "Guilty. For making love to me just now." She stood tall in the middle of the room, clad only in her blouse and lacy panties.

"Guilty? Vanessa, what would you do if you found out you were pregnant right now? Would you tell me?" he demanded, on the brink of anger, not sure if it was directed at her, or at himself for his lack of control in the situation.

"Michael, you should know me better than that," she said, the hurt expression flooding her pouty face. Her eyes glistened with tears nearly shed. "I love you, too."

He closed the distance between them with two smooth steps, gathering her up into his arms, smelling the sweetness of her damp hair. He kissed her head, then pulled her shoulders away from him, to look into her eyes.

"I don't know what you would do in that situation, Vanessa. It is frightening to think I could lose you if you felt you couldn't tell me. I don't even know if you want children," he said, vexation pulling at his finely carved face. "Why didn't you and Mark ever have any children?" he asked.

The hurt expression in Vanessa's face made Michael almost wish he had never asked. He wanted to reach down and wipe the trickle of tears that fell from her green eyes. "We never really discussed it, but Mark loved the business so much, and spent so much time with it, that when he was home, he said he didn't want to feel tied down with babies running around. I never pushed the issue, hoping that someday he would change his mind. I wanted children to fill the void in my life, but when we finally agreed to try, we found out Mark was sterile. He seemed to hate to touch me after he found that out."

"Do you still want children, Vanessa?" Michael asked, pulling her gently toward him to cuddle and protect her in his embrace.

"Yes, oh, yes. But the way my life has been going, who knows if I'll ever have a chance to—what with running the business now and everything." She shrugged, pulling herself away from him to gaze into the intense gray eyes she grew to adore.

"Michael, if I did get pregnant I would tell you. I just wouldn't want you to feel trapped into marrying me if that happens. I know how you feel about making that commitment. I want you to know I understand how you feel."

"But what would you do if you were pregnant now? Leave the business? Keep working? What?" He held his breath, fearing an answer he couldn't work with.

"I'd want to keep busy with something," she said, not sure what it was just yet. "Why don't we just wait and see? Then we can make that decision. In the meantime, let's go for dinner. I'm starving."

Michael was satisfied with her answer for the moment, sensing the topic was closed for now. "I want a big family," he said, as he tapped Vanessa on the behind as they headed out the door.

Michael followed her out the door, watching her as she walked gracefully in front of him to the elevator, the heels of her cream pumps sinking neatly in the plush hall carpet. She would work, he was sure of it. Even if she did sell the business. There was nothing that would stop this woman from doing what she wanted to do, not even his child, he thought, as the elevator door closed behind them.

They made a trip up the Squamish Highway, driving all the way into Whistler. The scenery was breathtaking from the top of the mountain. They spent an hour on top of Whistler Mountain before taking the gondola back down to the base of the village. Vanessa had never seen such natural beauty as she vowed to learn how to ski next winter.

They played the part of tourists for the rest of the week, taking the BC ferry from Tsawwassen to Sydney, on Vancouver Island. The drive into Victoria was quick, with the flow of traffic speeding into the middle of the city, dispersing more as they neared the downtown core.

Vanessa found she had forgotten to check on the stores she had in Vancouver while she and Michael busily planned their days during breakfast in the cozy hotel suite or restaurant. The nights were filled with concerts and sight-seeing. Vanessa had never had a vacation like this one, so fun-filled and enjoyable. Michael seemed to have a knack for surprising her when she least expected it. If it wasn't a bouquet of flowers ordered with breakfast, it was a hot air balloon ride.

The room he booked in the Empress Hotel was magnificent, overlooking Victoria Harbour. Vanessa enjoyed the ocean view. The last time she stayed here, the only room left was on the back of the building, overlooking the bus station. The whole vacation had been so much fun, she felt guilty asking Michael for half a day off, to visit the new warehouse Jason had found for her.

He wasn't too thrilled, but finally gave in when Vanessa suggested he visit the Antique Car Museum since she wasn't interested in it. The separation would be a perfect opportunity for them to take a break from each other for the afternoon before having to head back to Vancouver to fly home again.

She tried to conceal the excitement she felt when he dropped her off at the warehouse. She felt guilty for wanting to mix business with pleasure, especially since it was mostly at Michael's expense, although she managed to pay for a few meals. She hopped out of the car after giving him a quick peck on the cheek, and agreeing to meet him in two hours here.

The outside was not great to look at, she thought, a little dismayed, but it didn't discourage her from walking right in, unannounced.

Her eyes adjusted quickly to the dimness of the expansive warehouse. Steel beams, dirty from neglect, held the framework together. The railroad tracks ran the length of the building, entering one door and exiting at the far end. In the far corner stood the only sign of habitation. She immediately recognized the medium-built man who stood behind the obtrusive wooden desk, seemingly occupied with a mechanical problem.

He looked up from his work an instant before she reached him. "Vanessa, I wasn't expecting you," Jason said, surprise echoing in the empty building.

"I didn't tell anyone I'd be here. What are you up to?" she asked, turning a full circle, opening her arms to emphasize the barren surrounding that she expected to be almost completed into proper storage for the stock that was destined to arrive in the next few months.

Jason quickly dropped what he was doing to stand in front of the desk, trying unsuccessfully to conceal the computer software package and materials he had spread out on the makeshift desk. He had not had a chance to discuss with her the computer package he had bought to control their inventory for all stores from the warehouse. Now she was facing him, peering over his shoulder at the package lying on the desk.

Jason was quick to explain the progress he had made in getting things ready to begin restructuring the inside of the warehouse in the next week. But Vanessa persisted, wanting to know all the details of the inventory system he was working on.

"I was only playing with it here. It isn't hooked up into the stores' systems yet," he started to explain.

"I should hope not. I never approved anything like this, Jason. Just what are you up to?" she demanded. The coldness in the warehouse reflected her sudden chilly approach to his efforts.

"Let's have coffee someplace where I can explain it all to you. I think you'll agree with me once you see how everything will work." He quickly hustled her out of the main door, locking it with the padlock he carried in his pants pocket.

"Next time you have a bright idea, run it by me first," she

said, holding her cup for the waitress to fill again. Jason nodded, waiting for her to finish what she had to say. After all, he was working for her, and she was right in demanding to know everything first.

"Vanessa, I have something to propose to you," he said, watching her eyes as she studied his face.

"Yes?"

"I was thinking, if I paid for the software system to go into all the stores, would you be willing to consider selling me shares in the company? I know I could have a future here; there's so much potential. But I want to get what I feel I'm worth, if I'm going to put in all the effort."

Vanessa tried to hide the smile that pulled at her lips. He certainly was sure of himself. "You don't think what you are doing is part of the GM's job?" she asked, watching him fidget with the napkin in his hand. "As GM it is your decision as to whether it would benefit the company or not. I agree with your idea of putting the system into all the stores, but that is an expense that I have to consider fully before going ahead. Obviously you want my job and yours." She watched him for a moment before continuing, scrutinizing his reaction to her words. The sudden thought of losing total control of the company made her uneasy, but she had an idea.

"I am thinking of selling the business. If you are at all interested, I'd like to discuss it with my lawyer to see what would be an agreeable sum."

Jason nearly choked on the mouthful of coffee, as his eyes widened. "You mean it? You want to sell? Why?"

"Personal reasons, actually." She didn't want to divulge too much, knowing it would probably beat her back to the office, and she wanted to tell the staff herself. "Are you interested?"

"Of course. But I'm not sure I can afford it right now," he said, his eyes meeting hers with an expression of hopelessness.

"I'm sure we can work something out. I'll be in touch."

They shook hands, talked for a few minutes while she

waited for the taxi to arrive. She waved happily, feeling that a weight had been lifted off her shoulders. Jason would succeed at the business, she assured herself.

She was excited to tell Michael that evening, but when she arrived at the hotel to find him in a somber mood, she was hesitant. Maybe after dinner she could find a way of bringing up the subject. After all, he hadn't proposed yet. What would she do if he didn't ask her? She pushed the thought to the back of her mind. She loved him, and she knew he loved her, and somehow everything would work out, she was sure. She wasn't relinquishing total control of the company to Jason, but it would give her the freedom to pursue her dream of owning a race horse or a riding stable if she worked at it.

"Michael, I've been thinking," she started, as they sat down at the elegant table in the hotel's dining lounge.

He looked up, smiling at the woman he adored. He wondered why it was so difficult to do what he wanted to do at this very moment. The tiny gift that was concealed in his suit jacket pocket poked him as he shifted his weight in his seat, reminding him that it was now or never. Vanessa would be returning to Prince George in the morning and his chance may never come again.

"So have I," he said. "About two things actually. The first one is difficult because I know how you feel about your business, but I want you to know that I'm buying Tea Bag."

Vanessa stared, totally unprepared for what he said next.

"I want him to be yours. You had told me once that you always wanted to own your own racehorse, and I think that little guy has potential." He studied her face as she lowered the coffee cup to its saucer.

"Michael, I have no place to raise a racehorse," she exclaimed, surprised that he would even think of buying her a horse. He didn't even know that she was selling the business, she realized, suddenly feeling lost, not knowing where to start.

"That's the second thing," he said, producing a tiny wooden music box from his pocket. Vanessa looked at it, then at his tanned face, his gray eyes watching her closely.

"Will you marry me?" he asked, opening the lid to the tiny box to expose the most beautiful emerald stone she had ever seen. The green reflected the colour of her eyes. The diamonds sparkled around it, making prisms of light dance in the evening glow.

"Michael," she started before the tears got in the way. "I have to tell you something first."

"I need to know if you'll marry me first," he said, an anxious feeling rising in his stomach. He didn't know if he had the courage to accept a negative response.

"Yes," she whispered. She allowed him to slip the ring onto her finger, squeezing her fingers gently before releasing them.

"I know it'll be hard, but I'd rather live with you part of the time, than not at all. Maybe you can arrange it so that you only work in Prince George when I'm out of town. We'll make it work," he said.

"Michael, I've decided to sell shares," she blurted out. "Jason is more than interested, and if it works out, I could have a very tidy sum, but with the relocation of the head office going to Victoria, I'll be farther away from you in Blue River than before." She stared into the gray depths that threatened to drown her in love. Taking a deep breath she continued. "We could start our own stable of thoroughbreds. With the money from the business, you wouldn't have to work out of town at all. You could come with me when I had to make my visits to the stores, and head office." She watched him, instantly aware of his shoulders straightening up, his neck tensing.

"I'm not going to live off your money," he said, pushing the last of his meal aside.

"Michael, that's not what I meant. We could make it work together. You just said you bought Tea Bag. That's a perfect start." Confused, tears welled up in her eyes, forcing her to either shed them right there or run for the washroom. Either one was ungraceful, but she opted for the latter.

"Tea Bag is for you," he insisted, unable to grab her wrist as she raced past him, bumping the table in her hasty retreat.

He picked up the bill, and headed out quickly. He'd be damned if she was going to run his life for him. He decided to take a long walk along the harbour, try to work out his frustrations, wondering what to do next. She certainly had a way of throwing things for a loop, he thought, as he stalked out of the hotel and headed for the wharf.

Why couldn't he see that she wanted him with her all the time, she wondered as she quietly knocked on the hotel room door. She had spent so many lonely nights waiting for Mark. Having the money from the business would make it so much easier for him to quit his consulting business, to have the time to spend with the horses he so obviously loved. They would have more time to spend together, doing something they both loved. Why did he have to be so stubborn?

There was no response to her knock. Remembering she had a second key in her purse, she searched for it. Maybe he couldn't hear her, she thought, as she made her way into the darkened room.

Her hand swept across the light switch with ease, as she entered the main part of the hotel room. He wasn't there. Panic rose in her throat. Maybe he already left her. Her eyes scanned the floor for his belongings. They were still there, she discovered, with relief. It took great courage for him to ask her to marry him, she thought, recalling what he had said about his former marriage.

She felt the sharp edge of the stone as it dug into her palm, as she held the wooden music box in her hand. But he had proposed. And she had ruined it, making him think they would live off her money. She should have guessed he would be a more traditional man on the inside. It was obvious that it was his pride that was in the way, she thought, her anger rising in her tight stomach.

She had to find him. She tossed the box on the bed and headed out, slamming the door in frustration behind her. It was dark. The chill of the air blowing off the ocean tossed her untied locks around her face. She shook her head to clear her vision. Still wearing the flimsy dress she had put on for dinner, she walked the length of the sidewalk in front of the Empress, wrapping her arms around herself for warmth. She searched as far as she could see in all directions, unable to spot him. Not knowing what else to do, she wandered down to the dock, to listen to the soothing sound of the waves lapping against the cement wall.

It was getting quite chilly now that the sun had fully sunk out of sight. Vanessa tried to control the shivering that racked her body. She wasn't going to give up, not until she found him, she thought, determination glinting in her eyes. She strained to find any sign of him along the quiet walkway. She finally had what she wanted, she thought, and through her own stupidity, she let him get away. Unable to search any further through blurring eyes, she sat heavily on the nearest park bench. She buried her head in her hands, unable to stop the uncontrollable tears.

The lamplight above the walk cast a dark shadow on the looming figure that walked silently toward her, stopping a mere five feet in front of her.

She jumped in sudden fear of the huge bulk standing over her. She knew better than to be out alone in a strange city. Her heart pounded as he reached for her, pulling her close with one arm around her waist, the other covering the soft waves of her hair.

Relief flooded her face as she recognized him. "Michael, I'm sorry," she said, not quite sure what she was apologizing for, but not knowing what else to say. She wanted him so badly, to have him forever, she would have said anything that would make him see that everything was going to turn out all right.

He was silent for a long moment before letting her go. The golden sheen of her hair reflected from the lamplight, giving her the angelic quality he knew she possessed. He couldn't believe he had hurt her with his reaction at dinner.

"No," he said, huskily, "I should apologize. I had no right to say such a thing to you." His shoulders slumped. His voice quivered. "Will you still marry me?" he asked, almost afraid of the answer.

She beckoned for him to sit down beside her. "Only if you will listen to me first." She sucked in the cool ocean air, steadying her nerves so she could continue clear-headed.

Michael nodded, taking the seat beside her. He turned to face her, keeping his distance, fearing any contact with her body would dilute his senses.

"If I married you, it would be with the understanding that we did not spend time away from each other. I went through six years of having a husband who was away more than he was home. I couldn't do that again." She studied his intense, dark eyes as they roamed over her upturned face.

"But that would mean you would have to give up your business as well. Are you sure that is what you want?" he asked.

"No, I'm not selling it. I'm selling shares to Jason. His enthusiasm for the company will only make it easier for me to relinquish some control. I could run my part of the business from any location, just by being linked by computer. I don't have to leave the ranch if I don't want to. Of course, I would still have to visit the stores at least once a year." She held her breath, waiting for his outburst.

"Maybe I could arrange my seminars around those dates and we could travel together."

"Oh, Michael, that's an excellent idea. Neither of us would have to give up our business completely. Why didn't I think of that?"

"Because I drive you crazy when I'm around you and you can't think straight," he teased.

She leaned into his masculine warmth, cuddling under his outstretched arm.

"I think you're right."

"Does that mean we've reached an agreement?" he asked, lifting her chin in his strong hand.

"Of course, if you think it's going to work."

"With you, I know it'll work. Let's head back," he said,

removing his jacket to cover her almost bare shoulders. "You're going to catch pneumonia."

Vanessa walked in the comfort of his arm draped over her shoulder. The clouds that threatened to burst all evening finally allowed a sprinkle to fall, freshening the grass and sidewalk with its dewy smell. But she refused to let the rain dampen her spirits. By the time they reached the Empress, the rain was pelting down, soaking them both to the bone. They rushed into the lobby and up the elevator.

"Let me draw a hot bath for you," Michael said, visibly worried by Vanessa's constant shivering. She sat huddled on the bed with the spread pulled around her shoulders. Her teeth chattered in protest.

"I'll be okay. I'm just cold."

He slowly removed the spread, helping her to her feet, to get the clinging damp clothes off. He helped her into the warm tub filled with her favorite bubble bath that she had packed along. The colour was returning to her cheeks, he noticed with a sigh.

He gently closed the bathroom door behind him after glancing at her lean body as she stepped into the warm tub. He removed his damp clothes and hung them up in the sleeping area of the finely decorated room. He grabbed a towel that was lying on the bed as she called from the bathroom.

"Michael, can you come in here for a minute?"

He poked his head in the door to see what she wanted. The soft contours of her shoulders peeked out of the foamy whiteness.

"I need you to wash my back," she said, beckoning him to enter. His tanned torso emerged. A white towel was draped around his hips making his desire for her obvious when he came into full view. She laughed and she grabbed the towel as he reached to retrieve a wash cloth from the rack above the toilet.

"Hey," he said, grabbing at the towel she still held in her hands. It was his mistake to reach for it, because she was faster than he was. She grabbed his lean leg and pulled him off balance, landing with a splash in the tub with her.

"You take your chances parading around like that," she said, her eyes gleaming with heated desire.

"No," he said, laughing, "it's you who's taking your chances," pulling her soaking body on top of his, relieved to see that she was feeling much better than when they first entered the room.

Eleven

"Thank you, Robert," she said, extending her hand as she rose to leave her lawyer's office. She could hardly keep from jumping up in her excitement. The deal was finally finished. Jason was her new general manager, with a substantial share in the Ballerina Music Box Company. She still had controlling interest, but the bulk of the decisions were now in Jason's hands.

"Good luck to you and Michael," he said, smiling at the beautifully-dressed woman who had occupied his office more than enough times in the short four years since he had taken over her legal matters.

"Thanks. I'll be in touch." He watched her as she walked to the door. In one graceful movement she exited, head held high. "Lucky guy," Robert said, as the door softly closed behind her.

Vanessa headed to the store in time to take Janice out for lunch. It was her last day of working in Prince George, and Vanessa had planned a quiet surprise party for her friend.

"You really don't have to take me out. It's not as if we won't be seeing each other anymore. Jason has assured me I can have all the time I want to visit with you and Michael on the ranch.

"I know, but I want to." She tried to conceal the mischievous grin as she guided Janice to her little sports car parked behind the building.

"I'm going to miss it here," Janice said, closing the car door behind her.

"So am I." Vanessa looked at her friend and smiled. "Guess we both got lucky."

"Yeah." Janice rubbed the ring that sparkled on her left hand. "So when are you and Michael going to come visit Jason and me in Victoria?"

"Just as soon as I get settled in the house we are going to Vancouver to pick up a new colt."

"How's Tea Bag doing, by the way?"

Vanessa warmed at the thought of her favorite horse, envisioning him as he ran around the corralled area in Blue River. "He's growing like a bad weed. Michael said he's going to be a fine racer with all the spirit he has in him."

Janice smiled, knowing how much Tea Bag meant to her friend.

"Here we are," Vanessa said as she pulled in front of the restaurant.

"But it says closed," Janice protested.

"That's because we wanted it that way." Vanessa pushed her friend inside in front of her as the room broke into a loud cheer. The streamers hung from the ceiling. The banner stretched across the section read, "Good luck, Janice."

Turning around to face her friend, Janice covered her mouth with both hands before bursting into tears. She threw her arms around Vanessa's neck, and whispered, "I'm gonna miss you so much. Thank you." Vanessa replied with a silent hug in return, fighting to keep the misty tears from spilling down her own cheeks.

The final connection had been hooked up in what used to be Michael's grandmother's bedroom. Vanessa rearranged the top of the desk, filling the drawers with the files she had brought when the head office was finally relocated to Victoria several weeks ago. Living on the ranch, she found so many things to divert her attention away from the business that she was feeling guilty.

Vanessa did nothing to change the atmosphere of the quaint room, except to put the big oak desk she took from her old office in the corner of the room across from the gabled window. It was going to be a challenge keeping up on the business from their ranch in Blue River, but she was all for giving it a try.

She was thankful that Michael had agreed that she set up an office on the ranch, making the transition from business woman to wife less difficult. She let Jason run most things now, keeping her informed on a weekly basis through the computer, although she had access anytime she needed it. She sighed as she sat back in the big black leather chair, gently stroking Charlie's back.

The now familiar pounding of six feet woke her from her dozing. Before she had a chance to retreat, the door was flung open and Major bounded up into her swelling lap.

"Down boy," Michael commanded, pulling at the over-grown pup's collar.

Vanessa laughed as Major's overly ambitious greeting caused papers to go flying with a sudden swish of his tail. "I wonder if he'll ever settle down and treat me like you," Vanessa said, as she released Charlie so he could hide under the brass bed.

"How's Tea Bag?" she asked, curious if he had given him his workout this evening or not.

"He's fine," Michael said, settling himself on the arm of the oversize chair she was sitting on. "I think we'll have a great racehorse there in a few years. He's as hyper as old Danny Boy used to be as a colt."

Vanessa reached up from her chair to smooth the piece of hair that never seemed to find its place behind his ear. "I'd like to see him tomorrow. I've been so busy setting up in here I don't know what it's like outside anymore."

"You don't have to know what's going on outside, as long as I'm here," he said, his voice low and familiar. He reached to release the holder that held her below shoulder length hair off her glowing face. Gently he pulled the soft tresses around her shoulders, smoothing back the soft bangs that always smelled like fresh daisies.

Michael offered his hand to help her out of the chair. He made a groaning sound, teasing her that she was a heavy-weight he had to deal with. He pulled her softly rounded body into his, gently placing his hand on her growing belly. His deep gray eyes glowed softly in the dimness of the unlit room. Six months ago he never would have thought that having a baby would affect him the way it did. Vanessa had become pregnant on their honeymoon, and he was glad it had happened sooner than they anticipated, he thought with warm satisfaction.

Vanessa warmed to his touch on her growing belly, feeling the baby move slightly as she stood beside her husband. She couldn't remember a time when she was so happy, so content with her life. Because of Michael, she thought, she had discovered more to life than she ever imagined, and looked forward to the future when they would be a family.

Major raced out the door in hot pursuit of Charlie, who tried to make a fast getaway. Quickly Michael closed the wooden door with a swift kick of his foot, backing Vanessa onto his grandmother's squeaky old bed, grabbing the opportunity to make love to his wife whenever the mood struck him, which seemed to be more often than he ever thought about when he first met her.

"You're going to regret leaving this bed in your office," he said, teasing her with his gentle nuzzling at her neck.

"No way," she said, returning his kisses with all the love she possessed.